Praise for

"Balaban unleashes hilarious McGrowl. . . . Filled with absurd humor and fun, cartoonlike action."
— *USA Today,* review of
McGrowl #1: *Beware of Dog*

"Mr. Balaban takes his obvious love of language and wordplay and creates a magical tale of a mind-reading dog that all young minds should read. An intelligent and plentiful debut."
— *Jamie Lee Curtis*

"For anybody who has ever had a dog, loved a dog, or wanted a dog. A great adventure beautifully written. I hope Bob writes the next one about me."
— *Richard Dreyfuss*

Read all the books about

#5

IT'S A
DOG-EAT-DOG WORLD

Bob Balaban

A Storyopolis Book

AN
APPLE
PAPERBACK

SCHOLASTIC INC.
New York Toronto London Auckland Sydney
Mexico City New Delhi Hong Kong Buenos Aires

To Mariah,
for your help and inspiration

ISBN 0-439-43458-0

12 11 10 9 8 7 6 5 4 3 2 1   4 5 6 7 8 9/0
                                              40

Printed in the U.S.A.
First printing, September 2004

CHAPTER ONE
Let the Games Begin

Thomas Wiggins woke up and rubbed the sleep from his eyes. He climbed out of bed, shuffled to the window, and stared out at the crisp fall morning. He considered his Sunday afternoon options. His best friend, Violet Schnayerson, had to go to her cousin's birthday party in Lower Cedar Springs and would be gone for the better part of the day. So much for lunch at the Schnayersons'.

If Thomas played his cards right, he could probably get his dad to drive him to the library over in Wappinger's Falls. He needed to look

1

up some facts about Ulysses S. Grant for a history paper that was due on Tuesday. Just thinking about homework made Thomas want to jump right back into his warm, cozy bed.

On the other hand, he *could* always go to the movies with Lenny Winkleman. That would definitely be more fun. Unless Lenny got sick and had to stay home. Lenny was nice, but Lenny was a hypochondriac. He was always getting over something. Or coming down with something. Or about to come down with something.

Just when Thomas was thinking about going back to sleep, his dog, McGrowl, woke up. The golden retriever yawned, stretched his long furry body, shook himself mightily, and sent Thomas an urgent telepathic message: *Want to visit Miss Pooch. Now. Miss her. Let's go. Please?*

From his spot beside Thomas's bed, Mc-

IT'S A DOG-EAT-DOG WORLD

Growl whined gently and looked up at Thomas with his most soulful expression. Of all the dog's amazing abilities, the telepathic connection he shared with Thomas was certainly the boy's favorite.

The Miss Pooch in question was the Schnayersons' dog. She was half bulldog and half Chihuahua. A bullwawa, as Alicia, Violet's older sister, liked to say. Miss Pooch had an undershot jaw, bloodshot eyes, and spiky fur that bristled all over her body. She always looked as if she had just stuck her paw into a light socket.

McGrowl preferred Miss Pooch to any of the other dogs in the neighborhood. Thomas couldn't imagine why. But as Thomas's mother frequently said, "There's a pot for every cover, and a cover for every pot." Thomas wasn't exactly sure what it meant, but if McGrowl was a pot, then Miss Pooch certainly was his cover.

"Breakfast time!" Mr. Wiggins called up from the kitchen.

McGrowl bounded out of the bedroom and down the stairs without a second's hesitation. Now it was Thomas's turn to send McGrowl a telepathic message.

Slow down, pal. You'll scare my dad, Thomas thought as he threw on his clothes and ran to catch up.

McGrowl put the brakes on immediately and skidded into the kitchen. He nearly knocked over a stool, terrifying poor Mr. Wiggins, who looked up in alarm and stifled a scream for help. Thomas's father was absolutely terrified of dogs. He tried to pretend he wasn't. He wasn't fooling anybody.

Mr. Wiggins knew McGrowl was a good dog. After all, it was McGrowl who had saved the lives of Thomas and Violet that rainy afternoon. Mr. McCarthy had suddenly lost control of his delivery truck and had nearly run over both children. McGrowl rushed in to save the day, nearly losing his own life in the process.

What Mr. Wiggins *didn't* know was that after a visit to a villain disguised as a veterinarian and a chance encounter with Olivia the cat in a nearby power plant, McGrowl had developed bionic powers. The golden retriever could now run faster and jump higher than any dog in the world. He also had X-ray vision and superhearing. His telepathic connection with Thomas would have made the boy the envy of all his classmates, if they only knew.

But only Thomas and Violet were privy to McGrowl's secret abilities. And they had long vowed never to reveal them to anyone.

Unfortunately, someone else was also aware of McGrowl's special powers. A force of evil lurked in the shadows of the peaceful town of Cedar Springs, Indiana. The force of evil had a name. Actually, it had two names: Milton Smudge and Gretchen Bunting. Smudge and

Bunting had a plan. They would kidnap Mc-Growl and subvert his special powers to their evil purpose.

With a bionic dog in their clutches, the evil duo knew they could easily take over Cedar Springs, and then the world. It was up to Thomas, Violet, and McGrowl to make certain this never happened. The three friends had vowed to maintain eternal vigilance.

Thomas sat at the kitchen table and poked idly at his three-cheese omelet. He wondered when Smudge and Bunting would surface again. They had a nasty habit of showing up just when he thought they were gone for good.

Thomas's older brother, Roger, had eaten his power breakfast earlier and was at basketball practice, getting ready for next week's big game against Elwood High. The winners would be declared all-state champions, an honor Roger's team, the Salamanders, hadn't received for more than twenty years.

Thomas looked up quickly. He thought he had glimpsed a shadow creeping across the lawn outside the window, and he sent a telepathic message to McGrowl. McGrowl quickly scanned the area with his X-ray vision and relayed his response to Thomas: *Nothing to worry about.*

Their interchange had not gone unnoticed. Thomas's mother also maintained eternal vigilance, though of a different sort.

"What's the matter, honey?" Mrs. Wiggins asked Thomas, looking up from the paper. Mr. and Mrs. Wiggins were finishing their coffee as they wrestled with a particularly difficult crossword puzzle. "You've hardly eaten a bite of your omelet. Are you feeling all right?"

"Sure, Mom," Thomas replied cheerfully. "Just thinking about my history paper." As he spoke, he shoveled an enormous quantity of eggs into his mouth.

Satisfied, Mrs. Wiggins's attention returned

to the puzzle. "What's a twelve-letter word that means 'defiant of authority'?" she wondered aloud.

"I'd say 'Miss Pooch,' except that's just nine letters," Thomas joked. McGrowl looked up from his bowl of scrambled egg whites and liver snaps at the mention of his favorite doggie companion.

"Starts with an *r,* ends with a *t,*" Mrs. Wiggins added hopefully.

"I'd say 'recalcitrant,' and I'd be right," Mr. Wiggins announced proudly, and he went to the counter to pour himself and Mrs. Wiggins another cup of coffee.

"Thank you, darling," Mrs. Wiggins replied, filling in the difficult word.

"Great omelet, Mom," Thomas said, getting up from the table.

McGrowl gobbled up a few remaining crumbs from his breakfast bowl and followed

Thomas into the hallway. Thomas helped Mc-Growl with his new blue-and-yellow corduroy poncho before throwing on his own winter jacket.

"We'll be at Violet's," Thomas called to his parents. If he couldn't spend the afternoon with his friend, at least he could spend the morning with her. It didn't really matter what Thomas and Violet actually did together. The two friends never tired of each other's company. They could spend hours examining an anthill. Or trying to put together the crystal radio set Violet had gotten for Christmas. Or just watching cars go by — they always had fun.

"Don't forget your mittens," Mrs. Wiggins called out from the kitchen. "Winter, I'm afraid, is nearly upon us." She pondered the puzzle in her hands. "'Swift-running Australian bird with undeveloped wings,'" she continued. "Three letters."

McGrowl sent Thomas a quick telepathic message. "Emu," Thomas proudly answered, echoing McGrowl's response as they returned to the kitchen, fully bundled up.

Mr. Wiggins smiled proudly as Mrs. Wiggins filled in the letters. "Whoever is teaching you kids biology is doing one heck of a job."

Thank you very much, McGrowl replied telepathically. Only Thomas, of course, was able to receive the message. He grinned as he ran his fingers through the unruly mass of brown curls that tumbled onto his forehead.

And before Mrs. Wiggins could think of anything else to worry about, Thomas and McGrowl were out the door and halfway to Violet's house quicker than you could say "'eight-letter word for speed,' starts with an *a,* ends with a *y.*"(And, by the way, if you had said "alacrity," you would have been right.)

CHAPTER TWO
Bad Dog

Miss Pooch heard the familiar sound of Mc-Growl's footsteps as Thomas and the golden retriever approached the Schnayerson house. She yapped excitedly, leaped out of Alicia's arms, and ran out of the bathroom to greet her friend.

Unfortunately, Alicia had been bathing the unruly little bullwawa at the time, and Miss Pooch was covered from head to tail in sudsy dog shampoo. The shower cap she wore to protect her delicate ears had slipped down over her eyes and prevented her from seeing the vanity as she crashed into it, sending a collection of perfume bottles, nail polish, and assorted afterbath products flying in her wake. Somewhat dazed, she resumed her dash for the front door.

"What's going on in there, honey?" Mrs. Schnayerson called nervously from her bedroom.

"Nothing, Mom," Alicia shouted, frantically trying to clean up the mess on the bathroom floor.

"Sweetie, it would be great if I only had to clean the house once, for a change," Mrs. Schnayerson called back. Earlier that morning, Miss Pooch had decided to drag her breakfast into the front hallway and spread it all over the walls. It had taken poor Mrs. Schnayerson the better part of an hour to clean up the mess.

Mrs. Schnayerson ventured out of her bedroom just as Miss Pooch came racing around the corner. The two of them nearly collided. Miss Pooch looked Mrs. Schnayerson right in the eye and shook herself violently, sending billows of soapsuds flying everywhere. She was off in a flash.

"This must stop!" Mrs. Schnayerson cried futilely, stamping her foot and wiping soap bubbles from her hair and neck.

Miss Pooch had recently completed her third round of comprehensive obedience training. She had received the lowest grade in the history of the school. She refused to obey a single command. Her favorite afternoon snack was still Oriental rugs.

"Oh, Mom, don't be such a fuddy-duddy," Alicia chided as she raced down the stairs after Miss Pooch, who was in the entrance hallway.

The doorbell was ringing insistently. Miss Pooch barked hysterically and hurled her surprisingly resilient little body against the front door.

Alicia threw open the door. Thomas and McGrowl looked up as Miss Pooch, unable to stop herself in midhurl, went sailing out onto the front lawn. She landed, unhurt, on a bed of Mrs. Shnayerson's prize chrysanthemums.

McGrowl rushed over to make certain she was all right, while Thomas and Alicia looked on, smiling. Violet wandered in from the kitchen to see what all the fuss was about.

"It could have been worse," Violet said brightly, surveying the scene. "She could have broken Mom's new birdbath."

"The morning's young," Thomas joked.

"Come back inside right now, Miss Pooch!" Alicia called. The dog didn't even dignify the command with a response.

Mrs. Schnayerson arrived and stared numbly out at Miss Pooch, who was casually munching on a few hardy flowers that had survived her crash landing intact. "Either that dog goes, or I do." She sighed. No one was listening. Miss Pooch had suddenly caught sight of Olivia the cat, and was off and running.

McGrowl sent Thomas a telepathic question: *Can I go, too?* Before Thomas had a chance to reply — and the answer would have been an emphatic "no!" — McGrowl was galloping across the lawn and down the street, knocking over Mrs. Schnayerson's new birdbath in the process.

"Watch out!" Mrs. Schnayerson called out weakly.

"Sure thing," Thomas yelled back as he and Violet ran through the flower bed after McGrowl, gingerly avoiding the broken shards of birdbath.

"Let me know the minute Miss Pooch gets back," Alicia said. She headed briskly for her room to begin dressing for her cousin's birthday party.

"I'll send up a flare," Mrs. Schnayerson muttered under her breath. She picked up a brightly colored flyer that had been neatly placed by the door and shuffled back into the house. In the kitchen, she poured herself a second cup of coffee and glanced down absentmindedly at the flyer in her hands.

"Wait a goldarned minute," she said out loud. "This I've got to see." She pulled out her reading glasses.

CALLING ALL NAUGHTY DOGS! THIS MEANS YOU, the brochure proclaimed in bold red capital letters.

In the lower corner, a large finger pointed at a photograph of a small, vicious-looking dog. It looked so much like Miss Pooch that Mrs. Schnayerson let out an involuntary gasp. She reminded herself it was highly unlikely that her own bullwawa had posed for the flyer, and continued reading.

Tried the rest? Now try the best. At the Biddle Doggie Center for Obedience Training, we guarantee to turn your furry little devil into a little angel every time. Call today for a free introductory session. Our special weekend packages include behavior modification, grooming, and our unique "Shih Tzu shiatsu" massage that's just right for the overstressed pet. Your dog will never be the same. Don't delay!

Delay? Mrs. Schnayerson thought. *A herd of wild elephants couldn't stop me.* She raced out of the house, and ran down the block, scanning the neighborhood like a sergeant on patrol. She soon came upon Miss Pooch, Mc-Growl, Thomas, and Violet. Olivia stared nervously down at them from her perch atop the highest tree in the neighborhood.

While Miss Pooch barked loudly and leaped joyously up and down, McGrowl was shinnying up the tree using his superior powers of mobility. Thomas and Violet looked on anxiously as the cat edged farther and farther out onto the highest limb in a desperate attempt to avoid what appeared to be the inevitable.

Suddenly, Mrs. Schnayerson's voice came booming loudly from behind them. "Get away from that cat this instant, Miss Pooch!" she called. " I'm not kidding." Miss Pooch looked sheepishly at Mrs. Schnayerson and obeyed immediately. This was a tone you didn't dare disobey. Not if you expected to get dessert anytime in the next few years.

At least, Miss Pooch thought as she made her way to Mrs. Schnayerson, *my hero, Mc-Growl, is still on the case.* Indeed, the golden retriever was still making his way up the tree.

"Aren't you going to say anything to Mc-Growl, Thomas?" Mrs. Schnayerson demanded incredulously. Violet gave her friend a shove.

"Oh, sure," the boy began awkwardly. Thomas had never actually disciplined Mc-

Growl before. "You get down from there immediately," he called in his most serious voice. He hoped McGrowl would forgive him.

McGrowl wasn't used to getting orders. Especially from Thomas. He fired back a telepathic response: *I'm not going to hurt the stupid cat. I just want to scare her.*

Mrs. Schnayerson gave Thomas a dirty look.

"I mean it, McGrowl!" Thomas said emphatically. "Get down right now." And then he added a telepathic message: *Extra dessert tonight if you do.*

Miss Pooch couldn't believe her eyes. McGrowl was giving in without so much as a whimper. Or at least an audible one. She stared at Mrs. Schnayerson with contempt, bugged out her already bulging eyes, and growled defiantly. McGrowl sent her a telepathic message urging her to keep quiet.

They were in enough trouble already. Unfortunately, telepathic communication was lost on Miss Pooch.

"Don't make that sound at me, Miss Pooch," Mrs. Schnayerson scolded. "We're going home. Now! Move it!" Miss Pooch put her tail between her legs and scampered homeward.

Thomas headed home, and McGrowl followed close behind. Thomas beamed him a quick *You're in the doghouse, mister.* He hated making McGrowl feel bad. But every dog needed to be disciplined once in a while, Thomas reasoned. Even a bionic one.

CHAPTER THREE
Meet the Biddles

Within minutes, an excited Miss Pooch was being packed off to her emergency appointment at the Biddle Doggie Center for Obedience Training. "Don't be scared, Miss Pooch," Alicia said soothingly as she unzipped the dog carrier and motioned for the bullwawa to get in. "We'll be back to get you in a couple of hours." Miss Pooch wasn't the slightest bit afraid. She hopped right off Alicia's bed and into the sturdy simulated-leather carrier without being told a second time.

Miss Pooch loved to travel. The joys of new sights, sounds, and especially smells were not wasted on her. During last year's annual Thanksgiving trip to Milwaukee, she had managed to demolish Gramma Schnayerson's entire collection of rare Meissen china birds in one well-timed leap off the mantelpiece. By the time she had been caught and subdued, she had managed to devour most of the turkey, a large portion of string beans almondine, and all of the stuffing — before landing in a large bowl of mashed potatoes and giblet gravy. She had never had so much fun in all her life.

"I want you down here right now, Alicia," Mrs. Schnayerson hollered up from the front hall. She was determined not to keep the Biddles waiting for even a second. "And if that dog isn't in her carrier and ready to go . . ." Before she had a chance to finish, Alicia had whisked Miss Pooch downstairs and onto the driveway, where Mr. Schnayerson and Violet were waiting in the family station wagon.

Holding the traveling case, Alicia slid into the backseat next to Violet. Violet carried her cousin's neatly wrapped birthday present in her lap. She and Alicia would be driven to the party right after they dropped off Miss Pooch.

Mrs. Schnayerson strode briskly over to the car and got into the front seat beside her husband. No one said a word. Mr. Schnayerson's fingers drummed nervously against the steering wheel. *You can cut the tension with a knife,* Violet thought. She noticed Miss Pooch quietly eyeing the gift in her lap and carefully held it as far away from the dog as she could.

Mr. Schnayerson pulled out of the driveway. The Biddle Doggie Center was an easy five-minute drive from the Schnayersons', but from the look on Alicia's face you would have thought Miss Pooch was being sent to

Siberia. "I can't believe you're really going through with this," she said, biting her lower lip. Alicia looked as if she might burst into tears at any moment. "Miss Pooch hates to be left alone."

"I'm afraid Miss Pooch is just going to have to get used to it," Mrs. Schnayerson said calmly as she took out a pencil from her purse, unfolded a piece of paper, and started filling it out. A quick call to the Biddles had resulted in a faxed application form.

"Why does she have to go?" Alicia moaned. "She doesn't like strangers."

"She should have thought of that before she chased the cat," Mr. Schnayerson said tersely. It was the first time he had spoken since this morning's incident. He rather liked dogs. But not Miss Pooch. He was tired of the havoc she constantly visited on his life. *Why couldn't she be more like McGrowl?* he often wondered. McGrowl was a dog you could, well, get behind. Loyal. Friendly. Obedient. A nice solid citizen of a dog.

"I think you're all horrible," Alicia said, reaching into Miss Pooch's case and sneaking her a scrap of bacon she had saved from breakfast. "Poor Miss Pooch," she whispered, her chin quivering. "They don't really love you. But I do."

Miss Pooch had no idea what the fuss was about. As far as she was concerned, this was turning out to be one of her favorite days. Seeing McGrowl, chasing a cat, and then being taken for a drive while being fed bacon was hardly cause for alarm.

"I bet Miss Pooch will enjoy staying at the Biddles'," Violet said cheerfully. "Maybe she'll finally learn to behave herself."

Alicia turned on her sister so suddenly that Miss Pooch, in her traveling case, nearly slid off her lap. "You take that back," Alicia said, punctuating her retort with a swift pinch to Violet's leg.

"Stop that, girls," Mrs. Schnayerson warned. "We're already here."

They had pulled up to a welcoming, freshly painted house. A sign on the mailbox spelled out THE BIDDLES in gently rounded letters.

A white picket fence bordered a picture-perfect green lawn. A pair of matching antique brass lanterns stood gleaming at either side of a sunny yellow door. Everything about the house was neat and orderly. Even the curtains that hung in the windows were freshly pressed and newly laundered.

Poor Biddles, Violet thought. *Miss Pooch will destroy this place.*

Mr. Schnayerson got out of the car, opened the gate, and motioned for the rest of the family to follow. As they marched resolutely down the path to the front door, Miss Pooch stared eagerly out of her carrier, as if she were embarking on a great adventure. And indeed, she was.

IT'S A DOG-EAT-DOG WORLD

Mrs. Schnayerson rang the bell, and in a moment the door swung open and a jolly-looking middle-aged man stood before them. He had rosy cheeks, a large handlebar mustache, and small, bright eyes that twinkled merrily. Something about him reminded Violet of a West Highland terrier.

"Hello! I'm Hiram Biddle, but everyone calls me Hi," the man said in a booming, cheerful voice, ushering the family inside. "Right this way," Mr. Biddle continued as he led the Schnayersons to a small room near the front of the house. As he walked he made a series of agreeable grunts that Violet could swear sounded like barking.

Filing cabinets, a desk, a small couch, and four chairs filled the room. The walls were lined with a number of awards and newspaper clippings extolling the virtues of the Biddle Doggie Center. "Sit down, sit down," Mr. Biddle said cheerfully, extending a large hand that Violet couldn't help thinking bore a striking resemblance to a paw. Mr. Biddle had been around dogs so much, it seemed as if he were turning into one.

Mrs. Schnayerson had handed Mr. Biddle the application she had been filling out and Mr. Biddle sat behind his desk, reading the form intently. As he read he muttered several uh-huhs and a couple of oh, mys. At last, he looked up and spoke to the family.

"Looks like we've got a serious case of b-a-d d-o-g on our hands." He broke into an enormous smile. "And I know just what we're going to do."

"You do?" Mrs. Schnayerson said hopefully. "Really?"

"Absolutely," Mr. Biddle said confidently. "Nothing here a little positive reinforcement can't cure."

"You haven't met Miss Pooch," Mr. Schnayerson said dubiously.

As if on cue, the little dog began to yap.

"Let's see what we have here," Mr. Biddle said as he got down on his knees and crawled over to Miss Pooch's traveling case.

As he reached out to unzip it, Violet let out an involuntary "Oh, no." There was no telling what Miss Pooch might do if let loose in a stranger's house. But it didn't appear as if Violet had a thing to worry about. Miss Pooch emerged slowly, sniffed Mr. Biddle cautiously, and then proceeded to lick the tip of his nose. "Down, please," Mr. Biddle said firmly, looking the little dog squarely in the eyes.

Lo and behold, the bullwawa stopped licking, tilted her head to one side, and immediately sat down. She stared at Mr. Biddle, eagerly awaiting his next command.

The Schnayersons stared at one another in disbelief. "What's going on?" Violet wondered aloud.

"Why don't you all say your good-byes to

Miss Pooch?" Mr. Biddle said. Alicia gave Miss Pooch a big hug and handed Mr. Biddle the dog's favorite blanket, a box of her special liver treats, and her cuddle toy. Violet looked at her watch. It was getting late. Her cousin's party was about to begin. She gave her mother an anxious look.

Mrs. Schnayerson passed along the look to Alicia, who gave Miss Pooch one last embrace.

Mr. Biddle had walked the Schnayersons halfway to the front door when a tall girl who appeared to be about Violet's age came running around the corner and almost bumped into them. She smiled awkwardly.

"Less rushing, more walking, Binky," Hiram Biddle said cheerfully.

"Sorry, Dad," the girl said as she waved a quick hello to the visitors. She wore her brown hair in a long braid. She had a warm, friendly smile, rosy cheeks, and big blue eyes that twinkled as if she had just been told a wonderful secret. Violet liked her immediately and was about to introduce herself when the girl held out her free hand.

"I'm Binky Biddle," she said brightly. "I hate to meet and run, but one of the new arrivals isn't exactly housebroken yet." And then she was off and running, a roll of paper towels under her arm and a bottle of club soda in her hand.

"He will be soon," Mr. Biddle called out encouragingly to his daughter. "In all my years of obedience training, never once have I failed to housebreak a dog," he confided to the Schnayersons.

Violet didn't want to say anything, but Miss Pooch had lived with the Schnayersons for more than three years and they still hadn't been able to housebreak her.

"Do you honestly think you can help us, Mr. Biddle?" Mrs. Schnayerson asked. "We've tried and tried, and nobody has been able to do a thing."

"Call me Hi," came the confident reply. "And the answer is yes. Here, Miss Pooch!" he said, waving a slice of rare roast beef and walking backward into the living room. Miss Pooch took off after him like a homing pigeon.

"I really like the Biddles," Violet said as the Schnayersons let themselves out and walked back to their car.

"I feel sorry for them," Mr. Schnayerson said as he got into the car.

"You heard what he said, Daddy," Alicia countered, following him. "They're gonna teach Miss Pooch obedience. They never fail."

"Never's a big word, sweetie," Mrs. Schnayerson replied, sliding into the passenger seat. "We'll keep our fingers crossed."

Just as Violet was about to get in, she noticed Stuart Seltzer's dad's car heading down the street. Sure enough, it pulled up right in front of the Biddles'. Stuart got out with Franklin, his beagle. Evidently, Mr. Seltzer had gotten one of the Biddles' flyers under his door as well.

"You, too?" Violet asked her classmate.

"Yup," Stuart replied, smiling. "Franklin just ate my father's quarterly tax returns." The beagle looked up sheepishly. Shredded bits of paper still clung to his muzzle. He burped, and the smell of the recently digested documents filled the air.

"Well, good luck," Violet said, getting into the car.

"Same to you," Stuart said, heading for the front door.

"We'll need it," Violet replied as she slammed the car door. As Mr. Schnayerson pulled out of the driveway, Alicia kept her nose pressed against the rear window and looked back forlornly at the Biddles' house.

CHAPTER FOUR
The More, the Merrier

Stuart was knocking on the Biddles' front door when Esther Mueller and her Chihuahua, Rumpelstiltskin, sprinted across the lawn and joined him and Franklin. Rumpy, as Esther called the tiny animal, took one look at the beagle and started barking ferociously.

Poor Franklin was so frightened that he leaped up into Stuart's arms and began to shake violently. The door opened and Binky came out to greet the new arrivals.

"Hi," she said pleasantly, "I'm Binky Biddle. Is everything okay?"

"Oh, yeah," Stuart answered sheepishly. He was trying to disentangle himself from his terrified beagle. "He always gets scared around other dogs. He's Franklin. I'm Stuart." Stuart held out his hand.

"Who's the little dog with the big voice?" Binky wondered as she shook Stuart's hand and looked over at the tiny Chihuahua.

"She's Rumpelstiltskin Mueller. She's two and a half. I'm her boss," Esther announced proudly. She took a deep breath and continued speaking. "My name is Esther Mueller and I live at 223 West Olive and I enjoy world history and languages and my hobbies are macramé golf and whistling and when I grow up I plan to go into politics or investment banking." She wasn't even out of breath. Esther loved to talk. For her, even the simplest of questions was an invitation to let loose with more information than you would have thought humanly possible.

Just then, Sophie Morris's dog, Fluffy, came running over, wagging her tail happily. Sophie came tearing around the corner after her, screaming at the top of her lungs, "Heel, Fluffy! Heel!" Fluffy wouldn't have heeled if her life depended on it. She was, as Mrs. Morris frequently said, "obsessively independent."

When Sophie reached Fluffy, she said sternly, "Don't ever do that again." But Binky watched as Fluffy wagged her adorable tail and jumped up and down eagerly. Sophie immediately gave in. She picked up Fluffy and cooed into the dog's perky little ears. Fluffy obviously had Sophie wrapped around her two perfectly groomed front paws.

Suddenly, Binky and the rest of the kids heard a boy screaming for help. Ralph Sidell was being dragged across the front lawn by his dog, Willie, an enormous Irish wolfhound. The dog was taller than the boy and weighed nearly twice as much. Willie wasn't a bad dog. He just had trouble with limits. A lot of trouble.

"Boy, have you guys come to the right place!" Binky exclaimed as Mr. Biddle poked his head out the door and smiled.

"Hi, kids," Mr. Biddle began. "Think you could get those wild animals of yours to calm down for a second?"

Ralph, Sophie, Esther, and Stuart all wagged their fingers and, in their sternest voices, commanded their pets to sit. The dogs didn't pay them the slightest bit of attention. They continued barking, sniffing, and leaping about.

Mr. Biddle smiled patiently. He leaned over and looked Ralph's wolfhound right in his clear gray eyes. "Sit down," Mr. Biddle said in a calm but forceful voice. Willie stopped eating Ralph's shoelaces and sat down immediately. It was as simple as that. Ralph had never seen anything like it.

"You kids are going to have to learn to

teach those pets who's the boss," Mr. Biddle began. "Three important rules to remember: kind but firm, kind but firm, and last but not least, kind but firm."

"Better listen to my dad, you guys," Binky warned. "He really knows what he's talking about." Stuart, Esther, and Ralph nodded admiringly. Sophie took out the little notepad she carried everywhere and wrote down Mr. Biddle's instructions word for word.

"So let's hurry up and get all of your four-legged pals signed up for dog training," Hiram called as he headed back into the house. "Class starts in five minutes. Last one in the door's a rotten egg."

He didn't have to ask twice. The children crowded into the office with their dogs and filled out the necessary paperwork. Then they hurried off, petless, at least for the next five hours.

*   *   *

IT'S A DOG-EAT-DOG WORLD

The grandfather clock in the hallway was chiming five as McGrowl bounded down the stairs three at a time. He joyously rushed to the door to greet a weary Thomas, who had just returned from a hard day at the library.

"Slow down, McGrowl," Thomas said, smiling. "You're gonna trample me."

After the debacle with Miss Pooch and Olivia, Thomas had asked Lenny Winkleman to go to the movies with him. But Lenny was having a possible allergic reaction to some new socks his mother had just bought for him. "I can only wear one hundred percent cotton," he explained sadly to Thomas. "My mom got me a fifty-fifty cotton-nylon blend by mistake, and I think I'm getting a rash. With me, a rash could turn into anything. Last time, I ended up with tonsillitis." *Poor Lenny,* Thomas thought. *Nobody should know that much about their socks.*

So Thomas's father had driven him to the library, where he spent a quiet afternoon reading President Grant's autobiography. Thomas considered writing his *own* autobiography one day. He would tell the story of McGrowl's superpowers and how he, Violet, and McGrowl defeated a pair of evil villains who were trying to take over the world. Thomas wondered if he and his friends would, indeed, ever accomplish that daunting task.

"Did you miss me, boy?" Thomas asked. McGrowl sent back a resounding telepathic *yes.* Then he wagged his tail furiously and rubbed his head against Thomas's legs, nearly knocking him over. McGrowl always acted as if Thomas had been away on a worldwide cruise whenever he walked into the house. Thomas wouldn't have it any other way. He patted and hugged his friend with all his might, glad that there were no hard feelings after that morning's incident.

Suddenly, McGrowl looked up, distracted.

IT'S A DOG-EAT-DOG WORLD

He heard the distant sounds of familiar laughter. It was a haunting, wicked laugh. It reminded McGrowl of cold, bleak winter mornings. McGrowl telepathically transmitted the sound to Thomas. The boy and the dog wondered where the laugh was coming from.

They didn't realize that tucked neatly away in an ordinary house, on an ordinary block, right in the heart of Cedar Springs, the evil Milton Smudge and his accomplice, Gretchen Bunting, were enjoying a hearty chuckle over the prospect of imminent world domination.

"Shoes off, please," Mrs. Wiggins said breezily. "I just finished vacuuming. Dinner's at six-thirty. McGrowl, are those paws clean?" McGrowl barked a crisp affirmative as he and Thomas hurried upstairs to Thomas's room, the sound of mocking laughter still ringing in their ears.

CHAPTER FIVE
An Ill Wind

At a little after five o'clock, the Biddles' door opened and Binky poked her head out. "Hi, everybody," she said with a smile to the people on her doorstep. "My dad will be out in a second with your children's wonderful pets." Obedience class had just ended, and Traci Mueller, Penny Schnayerson, Art Morris, Elmer Sidell, and Gillian Seltzer stood, nervously waiting.

Everyone exchanged curious glances. Their dogs had been called a lot of different things, but "wonderful" was not usually on the list.

"No need to worry," Mr. Biddle announced as he joined Binky at the door. "Your animals have completed today's session with flying colors." Then he grinned from ear to ear, snapped his fingers, and whistled softly.

Willie Sidell emerged from the house, trotted gracefully over to Mr. Biddle, and sat obediently right in front of the man. Elmer Sidell's jaw dropped. Rumpelstiltskin, Fluffy, and Franklin were next. Each dog trotted out, sat down, and looked eagerly up at Mr. Biddle, waiting to be told what to do.

None of the owners dared to move, lest they break the spell that appeared to have been cast over their dogs.

"And let me tell you something about your bullwawa, Mrs. Schnayerson," Mr. Biddle began. Violet's mother bit her lip and prepared herself for the worst. "That clever little mutt was our star pupil. I don't think I've ever encountered such intelligence in a four-footed creature." Mrs. Schnayerson's eyes widened.

As if on cue, Miss Pooch came strolling out of the house, sat down at Mr. Biddle's feet, and waited obediently for her instructions. Mrs. Schnayerson regarded her dog with a mixture of awe and fear.

"You must take the reins," Mr. Biddle said patiently. "Your dog is a highly intelligent animal. She must learn who is in charge."

Binky looked on encouragingly. "Go ahead, Mrs. Schnayerson," she chimed in. "Miss Pooch needs you to tell her what to do. She really does."

Mrs. Schnayerson took a deep breath, leaned over, and summoned all of her courage before uttering the simple command, "Come here." Miss Pooch walked over, allowed her leash to be put on, and sat quietly at Mrs. Schnayerson's side.

Mrs. Schnayerson was amazed. "I just — I

can't — I don't —" she was so grateful she could hardly speak. "You people — how — what —" She continued spluttering as she led Miss Pooch to the car and got in. As she drove off, she rolled down her window and called out to the Biddles, who were standing proudly at the foot of the driveway, "How can I — when will you — what should I —" And then she was gone. Within minutes, four more happy dog owners had signed up for next weekend's refresher course and bundled their newly trained pets swiftly and peacefully into their cars.

McGrowl was playing a rousing game of hide-and-seek with Thomas in the backyard when he heard Miss Pooch returning to the Schnayersons'. His superhearing had immediately detected the jangle of her collar and her familiar "I'm home now" bark.

Please, can I go see Miss Pooch now? McGrowl begged. *I'll be good.*

"Sure, boy," Thomas happily agreed. After promising Mrs. Wiggins to be home in time for dinner, off they went.

They were halfway to Violet's when they noticed a handkerchief lying on the sidewalk. *Some nice old lady is probably wondering where she dropped it,* Thomas thought as he leaned over to get it. A sudden gust of wind picked up the kerchief, and it fluttered and danced out of his reach until it came to rest right on McGrowl's long, furry muzzle.

"I think that handkerchief likes you, pal," Thomas joked as McGrowl shook his head from side to side, trying to disengage himself from the persistent cream-colored square. The scent of a familiar, bitter odor clung to it and made McGrowl sit up in alarm.

"What is it, boy?" Thomas asked. Something bad was happening. Thomas sensed it immediately.

It's them, McGrowl thought. *They're back.*

"Are you sure?" Thomas whispered.

McGrowl let Thomas know his response with a determined look that practically screamed, "Yes, I'm sure!" The dog had immediately recognized the faint but distinct smell of formaldehyde and disinfectant associated with his nemeses.

Thomas picked up the handkerchief and immediately noticed the two initials neatly embroidered on the lower corner: *GB*. Gretchen Bunting. It was perfectly clear. The evil duo had made its return. "Bunting must have been spying on us and dropped it," Thomas said as he pulled his collar up around his neck and glanced around. "They could be watching us right now."

Night had fallen, and there was a cold, wet chill in the air. The thought of the devious marauders sent an icy shiver racing down Thomas's spine.

McGrowl scanned the area carefully. *We're*

alone, he reassured Thomas. *At least for now.* Thomas turned his attention back to the embroidered handkerchief. He and McGrowl sat on the curb and examined their surprise discovery.

Upon closer inspection, the kerchief revealed nothing extraordinary. Thomas searched it for a leaf, a strand of hair, anything that might possibly lead them to the whereabouts of their enemies.

McGrowl carefully studied the kerchief for evidence on the molecular level. Looking for fingerprints wasn't even an issue. As McGrowl well knew, fingerprints don't adhere to textiles.

The fabric, he quickly determined, was an ordinary machine weave, and there was nothing unusual about the monogram itself. It was an inexpensive handkerchief that could easily be found in any department store. No help there.

Then McGrowl noticed a brownish smudge

on the upper corner of the cloth. Closer inspection revealed it to be a common plant-based hair dye found in many drugstores and beauty salons. Perhaps Bunting had used the dye to color her hair and gotten some of it on her handkerchief.

A promising clue, McGrowl thought. He remembered Mrs. Wiggins had recently purchased such a product to cover up what she referred to as her "little gray intruders."

"What do we do now?" Thomas asked McGrowl, who quickly sent back a telepathic explanation. *If we can find the store that sells this dye, we might be able to uncover a clue that will lead us to Bunting.*

"What is it?" Violet asked as Thomas showed her the handkerchief. The three friends were huddled on Violet's porch, whispering urgently.

"We found it on the lawn in front of Mrs. Erickson's house," Thomas replied. "It's got Smudge and Bunting's telltale scent all over it."

"Are you absolutely sure?" Violet asked anxiously. McGrowl nodded his head.

"It's even got her initials on it," Thomas added as he carefully pointed out the delicately embroidered $\mathcal{GB}$ in the corner.

"And just when it looked like they were gone for good," Violet remarked wistfully.

"We're going to go looking for more clues. Want to help us?" Thomas asked eagerly.

"I can't," Violet replied. "I have to be here to help out with Miss Pooch. My mom has given up." Miss Pooch, it seemed, had reverted to her old behavior immediately after returning home from the Biddles'. She had eaten the fringe from the bottom of Mrs. Schnayerson's new drapes.

Thomas and McGrowl combed the neighborhood for a little longer and found no more clues. Not even a footprint.

"And where have you two been?" Mrs. Wiggins demanded when Thomas and McGrowl arrived back at the house. "Dinner's already on the table. I hope you like ice-cold mashed potatoes."

Fortunately, the usual "our ball got lost in the bushes" strategy worked just fine, and the rest of the evening unfolded uneventfully. Roger, exhausted from basketball practice and nursing what the coach had described as a "lightly strained" ankle, returned during dessert. He hobbled and hopped, soaked the lower half of his body in Epsom salts, and wrapped his entire leg in an enormous compression bandage. With the championship game less than a week away, he wasn't taking any chances.

Soon, it was ten o'clock and Thomas and McGrowl were in bed. As Thomas lay awake, lost in thought, McGrowl slept fitfully. He was having a nightmare about Smudge and

Bunting. They were dragging him away, attempting to fasten an electromagnetic collar around his neck.

The dog fought with all his might. If the villains were successful, he knew his superpowers would soon disappear and he would be in their clutches forever. His paws churned in the air as he tried in vain to push away the evil duo.

Thomas put a hand on his dog's head, trying to calm him. He studied the galaxy of tiny phosphorescent stars his father had painstakingly glued to the ceiling two years ago, for his eighth birthday. The shimmering discs reminded Thomas how insignificant his problems were in the face of the vast universe and gave him a reassuring sense of perspective.

Maybe this time the evil duo will go away for good, Thomas told himself. *And we can finally stop worrying once and for all.* By the time he had reached Canis Major, he, too, was falling asleep. His eyes closed and he began to dream that Smudge and Bunting were taunting him, laughing at his efforts to rescue McGrowl from their newest fiendish trap. Thomas sat up suddenly, wide awake and panting heavily.

"Just a dream," he said to himself, "nothing to worry about." He tossed and turned until just before dawn when, exhausted at last, he fell into a deep, deep sleep.

Outside, a gentle rain was falling. The early train out of Upper Wappinger's could be heard blowing its sleepy whistle as it rounded the bend on its way to Kokomo. Not so very far away, Milton Smudge and Gretchen Bunting peeked out from behind a tiny hidden window in the attic of their secret lair. They grinned wickedly as they watched the very same train wind lazily by. A new day was dawning. It was bringing them one step closer to their terrible, unavoidable plan.

CHAPTER SIX
A New Friend

It was Monday morning, and Thomas and Violet were waiting for the bell that would signal the beginning of first period science class. Several eighth-graders walked by dressed as Salamanders, chanting, "We hate Hippos." No one paid the slightest attention. With the big game against Elwood only six days away, acts of fanatical devotion were not uncommon. The rivalry between Elwood's Hippos and Stevenson's Salamanders was legendary.

Suddenly Gosling Fletch, their teacher, peered out from his classroom. He addressed the lingering students with a dramatic "Science awaits." Everyone filed into the room and took their places behind their desks.

"Open your textbooks to chapter seven, class," Mr. Fletch began. "And we shall immerse ourselves in the fascinating study of our beloved friends in the plant kingdom." Pages fluttered like butterfly wings as seventeen students turned to the chapter entitled "How Things Grow." Suddenly, Mabel Rabkin, Stevenson's ancient and beloved registrar, poked her wrinkly head into the classroom and addressed the group.

"Children, say hello to a special new student," Miss Rabkin said as she ushered a gangly young girl into the room. Violet looked up and immediately recognized Hiram Biddle's daughter, Binky. Violet smiled at her. Binky smiled back as the class issued a friendly round of hellos.

The new student wore a freshly pressed

khaki skirt and a crisp white blouse. She looked as clean and neat as a shiny new apple.

"Class, meet — meet — your name is on the tip of my tongue," Miss Rabkin said as she concentrated with all her might. "Or, at least, it was."

"Binky Biddle," Binky said softly.

"The tip of the old tongue isn't what it used to be," Miss Rabkin said, smiling. "But then, neither is the rest of me."

"Welcome to our humble classroom, Miss Biddle," Gosling Fletch said pleasantly. "What brings you to our fair city? Were you carried in on last week's meteorite shower?" He chuckled at his little joke. No one else did.

Miss Rabkin continued, undeterred. "She's traveled all the way from — where d'ya say you were from, honey?" Mabel inquired politely. Mabel was eighty-three, and although an excellent registrar, she did have her "senior moments," as she referred to them.

"I'm from Rapid City," the girl replied.

"Speak up, honey, the ears aren't what they used to be, either," said Miss Rabkin.

"Rapid City," the girl said, practically shouting now.

"Come again?" Miss Rabkin persisted.

The poor girl leaned over Miss Rabkin, cupped her hands around her mouth, and screamed directly into the older woman's ear, "RAPID CITY!"

"Well, why didn't you say so in the first place?" Miss Rabkin replied as she prepared to return to her office. "Be nice to her, kids, she's come all the way from Boston." And with that, she was off.

"I'm just here for the rest of the semester," Binky explained to the class as she took an empty seat near Violet and pulled her textbook out of her book bag. "My dad and I are moving to London in the spring."

Everyone was eager to hear all about the

new student with the exciting future and the friendly smile, but Mr. Fletch put two fingers into his mouth and let out an earsplitting whistle while pounding loudly on the desk with his right hand. The gesture, while quite startling, was merely intended as an efficient request for silence. It worked every time. The students stopped talking and turned to face their teacher, who rose dramatically from his seat and began to speak.

"I am a plant. I am green. I make my own food. My favorite word is *photosynthesis.* Tell me something I don't know." Mr. Fletch had a real knack for getting the students' attention. If his loud noises didn't do the trick, his provocative line of questioning certainly did.

"I believe your favorite word comes from the Greek," Sophie Morris gamely began.

"I knew that," Fletch said dryly. "What does it mean?"

Sophie continued, undaunted. "It means

taking pictures, um, of leaves, I believe. You do this by using the sun and, um, special paper found only in certain camera stores. A lot of people don't know this, but it also means the thing that happens to your retina when you look at a bright light too long." Sophie appeared to have read the chapter but had clearly failed to grasp the meaning of many of its finer points.

"I can feel my poor leaves withering. Is she right, class?" Mr. Fletch asked.

A loud chorus of no's rang out all across the room. Sophie looked extremely surprised and disappointed.

"And why not, Mr. Musser?" Mr. Fletch asked, suddenly pointing a long, bony finger at the startled boy.

"Because, um, things can only mean one thing?" Lewis replied tentatively.

Considering he had been playing with his Game Boy under the desk for the entire class and had never even bothered to open his textbook, there was a certain logic to his answer.

"Good answer, Lewis," Mr. Fletch said supportively. "But not, in this case, a correct one. Anybody else?"

Both Thomas's and Stuart Seltzer's hands shot up like arrows. "Yes, Mr. Seltzer?" Mr. Fletch asked.

"Photosynthesis," Stuart began, "is when plants combine energy from light with water and carbon dioxide to make food."

"Excellent," Mr. Fletch remarked. "My leaves are definitely perking up." He raised his hands high in the air and waved them about as if they were leaves before continuing his questions. "Does photosynthesis occur in mushrooms" — he paused for dramatic effect before selecting his next victim — "Miss Biddle?" A hush fell over the class.

IT'S A DOG-EAT-DOG WORLD

Was it fair, Thomas wondered, *to ask a newcomer such a difficult question on her first day of school?* He and Violet exchanged a worried glance.

"May I please take a moment to think about that?" Binky asked. She chewed her pencil and pulled at the end of her long braid. She scrunched up her face and looked anxiously at the ceiling.

Violet felt terrible for the girl. She quickly jotted down the answer on a scrap of paper and then realized that it would be impossible to pass it to Binky without being discovered. Every eye in the class, including Mr. Fletch's, was riveted on the new student.

"It seems to me," Binky tentatively began, "that mushrooms are usually white. Or cream colored. Or maybe even gray. But I can't recall ever having seen a green one, and I'm pretty sure only green plants can do photosynth" — she stumbled over the difficult word — "syntha . . . *synthesis,*" she finally said, relieved.

"So what, precisely, is your answer, Miss Biddle?" Gosling Fletch demanded imperiously. It was so quiet in the classroom, Violet could hear her heart thumping in her chest. Thomas was so nervous he shredded his eraser as he waited for Binky to respond.

"I would have to say that because mushrooms are white and don't contain, um, chlorophyll" — everyone held their breath and waited for her to continue — "and because chlorophyll is essential for that photo-whatever thingy" — Binky was too nervous to even attempt to pronounce it — "I would have to say that the *p* word does *not* occur in mushrooms."

"Is that your final answer?" Mr. Fletch demanded.

Binky thought long and hard. "I would have to say . . . yes," she finally replied.

"Louder, please," Mr. Fletch prodded quietly.

Binky pulled back her shoulders, stuck out her chin, and came forth with a resounding "Yes!"

"Congratulations," Mr. Fletch declared jubilantly. "You have both a correct answer and the courage of your convictions." The entire class broke into cheers and sustained applause.

Violet was pleased to discover that her first impression of the girl had proved to be an accurate one. Binky had shown herself to be a brave and immensely likable girl, as well as a determined, if not altogether accomplished, student of science. She was quickly on her way to establishing herself as the most popular girl in the middle school.

CHAPTER SEVEN
Warning Signs

Binky continued to beguile the middle school. Not only had she endured Mr. Fletch's grilling like a trouper, in second period she went on to receive the only A on Miss Thompson's pop English quiz and entertained the class with a stirring rendition of the poem "If" by Rudyard Kipling. By recess, there was already talk of her running for student council president.

Meanwhile, back at the Wigginses', Mc-Growl was trotting up the driveway. He had walked Thomas and Violet to the school bus, stopped briefly at the Schnayersons' to say hello to Miss Pooch, and spent a relaxing hour chasing Olivia the cat.

But McGrowl couldn't stop thinking about last night and the handkerchief. It was hard to have fun when you were constantly looking over your shoulder to see if a villain was trying to kidnap you.

McGrowl noticed Mrs. Wiggins struggling with a large bag of garbage. He ran to the back door and held it open for her with his head. "Thanks, McGrowl," Mrs. Wiggins said affectionately. The dog followed her over to a large aluminum container at the side of the driveway. He picked up its heavy lid with his powerful teeth and held it open while Mrs. Wiggins threw in the bag. "Don't know what I'd do without you," she said gratefully.

McGrowl looked up at Thomas's mother with his big brown eyes. If he could have, he would have smiled. Being useful was one of his favorite activities. It almost made him forget, for a moment, the danger he and Thomas were in.

He padded alongside Mrs. Wiggins as she retrieved a colorful flyer from underneath a pile of leaves by the door, and went back into the house. McGrowl would return to school in a few minutes, as soon as he finished his breakfast. He would wait outside the window of Thomas's classroom, keeping an eye on his boy. Given the events of last night, he wasn't about to let Thomas out of his sight for long.

McGrowl lay down next to Mrs. Wiggins and rested his large head on her feet as she sat at the kitchen table and absentmindedly removed bits of dried leaves from the flyer. He growled a soft growl of contentment.

He loved mornings at home with Mrs. Wiggins. When she was done with her coffee, she would pour whatever was left over into his bowl and place some toast or a piece of muffin beside it. Today's special treat was half a cinnamon bagel.

He carefully held the bagel between his teeth and dunked it into the coffee. Then he flipped it into the air, looked up, opened his mouth, and waited for it to land on his big, floppy tongue. He never missed.

"Will you look at this!" Mrs. Wiggins exclaimed as McGrowl eagerly chewed on his soggy treat. She was reading the flyer. "A school for naughty dogs. What a good idea! Why didn't I think of that?"

McGrowl looked up at her curiously as she studied the Biddles' brochure. Surely she didn't think *he* needed to go there. "Not for you, McGrowl," she said looking down and smiling. "You could probably teach the rest of us a thing or two." Sometimes McGrowl could swear that Thomas wasn't the *only* family member capable of reading his mind.

"I think it's time for me to go back to work, McGrowl. What do you think about that?" Mrs. Wiggins said casually as she went to the sink, rinsed her coffee cup, and put it into the dishwasher. She frequently used the dog as a sounding board. She would have been surprised, indeed, to discover he understood every word she was saying. As McGrowl pondered the question, Mrs. Wiggins unwrapped a fresh sponge and polished the tops of the already spotless counters until they sparkled.

"Yes, I believe it is," she said in a quiet but determined voice. And then she mentioned a few more things like "paying off the mortgage," and "two-income household," and "self-fulfillment." Meanwhile, she rolled out the refrigerator and started busily cleaning behind it. "I'd love to find something I could do at home," Mrs. Wiggins mused. "Something meaningful but . . . contained. Short hours, lots of flexibility — you know."

IT'S A DOG-EAT-DOG WORLD

But McGrowl *didn't* know. He stopped chewing and listened intently. As far as he could tell, Mrs. Wiggins was already working. In fact, McGrowl had never seen anybody work as hard as Mrs. Wiggins did. There was scarcely a moment in the day when she wasn't picking someone up in her car, or cleaning the house, or fixing a meal.

And then it dawned on him: Mrs. Wiggins was talking about a different kind of work. The kind of work that involved the thing that McGrowl had come to know as money. He had never actually had the opportunity to make use of the stuff himself. But he knew it was important to his two-legged friends. He knew it was frequently green and made out of paper. He also knew that people were generally happy to see it, although Mrs. Wiggins didn't seem to enjoy the hard and shiny kind when it ended up in Thomas's pockets and ruined the washing machine.

"Don't look so serious, McGrowl," Mrs. Wiggins said as she leaned down and gave him a hug. "No big deal. It's not as if I'm starting tomorrow or anything. We'll just keep our eyes open in case an interesting opportunity presents itself. Okay?" McGrowl nodded thoughtfully. "No big deal," she said again, which meant, of course, that it *was* a big deal. Even McGrowl knew that.

The dog watched as Mrs. Wiggins went upstairs to take all the laundry out of the hampers and the sheets off the beds. Monday was wash day. As she walked, she hummed. She appeared to be quite happy about her new idea.

It was then that McGrowl made up his substantial mind. If a job would make Mrs. Wiggins happy, then he would help her find one. And somehow McGrowl had a feeling it wasn't going to be all that difficult.

*　　*　　*

IT'S A DOG-EAT-DOG WORLD

By lunchtime, every single person in the fifth grade was vying for the attention of Binky Biddle. Most of Stevenson Middle and a good portion of the high school had heard all about Binky's exciting life as the daughter of a successful dog trainer, as well as her impending trip to London.

The cafeteria bustled with hungry students. At the center table, Violet occupied the seat of honor at Binky's right. Ralph Sidell sat directly across from the two of them, and little Esther Mueller took up the last available space at the foot of the table. Ten other lucky students occupied the rest of the seats.

"Tell me something, Binky," Esther asked in her most grown-up voice. She felt especially honored to be sitting at a table comprised entirely of fifth-graders. "I'd like to know A, how our school compares to your old one; and B, if the weather here is one, better, two, worse, or three, exactly the same as the weather in Rapid City; and C, most of all, how great is it to have all those dogs around all the time?"

Just as Binky was about to respond, Esther couldn't help asking yet another question. "And last but not least, D, could I have some of your applesauce?" Everyone laughed as Binky spooned a generous portion onto Esther's plate and began her lengthy explanation.

Thomas got to the cafeteria several minutes after the lunch bell had sounded. Usually, Violet reserved a special place for him right beside her. But by the time Thomas arrived with his peanut butter sandwich and his glass of milk, the lunchroom was so crowded, he had to sit at one of the smaller tables, between Lewis Musser and Lenny Winkleman. *Where is Violet?* he wondered.

At last, he spotted his friend at the center table and waved to her. She was too busy talking to Binky to even notice. Thomas tried not to pay attention to the unreasonable little stab of jealousy in the pit of his stomach. Even after he and Lenny had a lively discussion about the possibility of viruses on other planets, the uncomfortable feeling remained.

Meanwhile, over at the "cool" table, Binky had finished her answers to A and B and was just beginning C. Everybody at the table, including several sixth-graders wearing "Go Salamanders" beanies, stopped eating and leaned forward to listen with rapt attention.

"First of all, I love dogs," she began. "And it's really fun being in the obedience business. My dad probably knows more about training animals than anybody in the whole world." This pronouncement was greeted with a series of oohs and ahhs.

"He's really amazing," Violet chimed in. "Even Miss Pooch listened to him." She neglected to add that the wondrous effects of

Mr. Biddle's training had completely worn off the bullwawa.

Binky talked about how much she was enjoying Stevenson Middle School and how much she preferred it to Jefferson Memorial, or "Jeff," as everyone in Rapid City evidently called it. "At Stevenson everybody is so friendly," she enthused. "At 'Jeff,' everyone belongs to these clubs and sororities and stuff. It's really cliquey. Nobody even talks to you if you aren't wearing the right sneakers." Not that Binky was the kind of girl who *wouldn't* have worn the right sneakers.

By now the lunchroom was clearing out and Thomas had moved to a table closer to the center. He watched as everybody at Binky's table laughed uproariously at everything she said. He noticed that Violet was giving Binky all her gummy bears.

Thomas tried not to think about A, how much *he* liked gummy bears; B, how left out he felt; and C, how much he was beginning to resent the new girl. *I'm not being fair,* he told himself. *Binky hasn't done anything wrong.* And yet everything about the girl was beginning to bother him: the way she took in little gulps of air when she giggled, even the way she smiled.

Get a grip on yourself, Wiggins, Thomas told himself as he put his tray onto the conveyor belt and watched as it wound its way slowly into the kitchen. *You have more important things to think about. Like the fact that the evil duo may be after McGrowl right now.*

CHAPTER EIGHT
Dead End Ahead

The minute school was over, Thomas and McGrowl resumed their detective work. They set out on a tour of drugstores and beauty supply shops in the area.

Thomas had, of course, asked Violet to join them. They always did their sleuthing together. But Violet told Thomas that she had to help Binky with frog anatomy. "Thomas, she needs me," Violet had explained during last period. "They didn't even have biology in her grade at 'Jeff.' She's so nice, I can't just say no."

"That's okay," Thomas had replied. "I don't

mind." He couldn't very well tell his best friend he was jealous because she was doing a good deed for a new student. So he and McGrowl set off alone.

Mr. Harvey's Heavenly House of Hair turned out to be a complete waste of time. Their browns were too red, and the only vegetable dyes they sold were all in shades of yellow. McGruder's Drugs didn't even sell hair care products. Carl's Sundries and Notions had a big sign in the window that said CLOSED FOR REMODELING.

Two and a half hours of sleuthing turned up exactly nothing, and as they rode home on the six o'clock bus, Thomas looked uneasily out the window at the darkening sky. He put a protective arm around his furry friend. "Don't worry, McGrowl," Thomas said in his most comforting voice. "Everything's gonna be okay." McGrowl sent Thomas a similar telepathic message in return.

After a delicious dinner of chicken potpie and buttermilk biscuits, McGrowl helped Thomas with his homework in the den, while Mr. Wiggins did the dishes and a distracted Mrs. Wiggins stared out the kitchen window and thought about new job possibilities. "I'd really prefer to work at home," she murmured to herself, "but that's so limiting."

"Excuse me?" Mr. Wiggins asked, attempting to remove a particularly stubborn grease stain from one of the dishes.

"Oh, nothing, darling," Mrs. Wiggins replied as she went to the sink, got a fresh dish towel, and helped with the drying. *Surely there's something just right for me,* she thought. *But what?* Out of the corner of her eye, she noticed that McGrowl had wandered in from the den and was regarding her thoughtfully. Or maybe it was her imagination.

Soon dishes were put away, teeth were

brushed, pajamas were put on, and everyone had gone to sleep.

Mrs. Wiggins lay in her bed and looked up at the ceiling. Mr. Wiggins was dozing beside her, another crossword puzzle resting, half done, on his chest.

It was the quiet time of the evening when mothers review their day and do some of their best worrying. *I must remember to tell Thomas to wear heavy socks tomorrow. It's flu season,* she observed as she arranged the covers around her. *Hope the frost doesn't damage my azaleas. . . . I wonder if I remembered to turn off the oven.* She turned restlessly in her bed and resumed staring at the ceiling.

Mrs. Wiggins's mind wandered over to "the plan," as she had come to think of her job search. Henderson Goolrick, her former boss at the bank, had said she could have her old assistant manager job back whenever she liked, but that would mean she couldn't work from home.

She pulled the covers up higher over her shoulders. It was definitely getting colder. Soon it would be time to get out the storm windows and put away the screens. Mrs. Wiggins felt strangely as if *she* were one of the winter comforters that had spent the summer months tucked snugly away in the cedar closet in the hallway and were about to be taken out of their plastic covers and brought upstairs.

She started drifting off at last. As she teetered on the brink that divides waking and sleeping, during which we do some of our most creative thinking, she began to think about Jell-O, and its many exciting applications.

Perhaps it was because McGrowl had taken out a number of Jell-O boxes after dinner that evening and arranged them haphazardly on the floor near the kitchen table. When Mrs. Wiggins had picked them up, she wondered why the usually neat animal had left such a mess.

Or maybe it was because when she returned the boxes to their proper place in the drawer, she spotted several cookbooks lying rather conveniently on the counter. *It is as if McGrowl is deliberately trying to tell me something,* Mrs. Wiggins thought as she lay in bed. She dismissed the idea immediately.

Surely such intentions are well beyond the scope of any normal dog, she reasoned. But she couldn't help remembering that the books were opened to several intriguing recipes she had never seen before.

As Mrs. Wiggins tossed and turned, the recipes from the cookbooks flashed before her eyes in a dizzying tumble of fluttering combinations until one perfect, finished creation appeared in her mind's eye as clearly as if she were holding it in her hands.

It looked like a Popsicle but tasted like nothing she had ever known. It was sweet. It was fruity. It was intense. It had the appealing consistency of frozen Jell-O, and all the flavor of banana cream pie, her favorite dessert.

She sat bolt upright in bed, and announced her fabulous plan in a loud, clear voice. "Momsicles!" she proclaimed, waking Mr. Wiggins with a start. "I'll call them Momsicles! I'll manufacture them in the home," she continued. "We'll make a fortune."

"What's happening?" Mr. Wiggins asked with alarm.

"They'll be delicious, nutritious, and come in an easy-to-carry six-pack," Mrs. Wiggins explained, as if her husband could possibly understand what she was talking about.

"Honey, go back to sleep," Mr. Wiggins

mumbled groggily. "It's the middle of the night."

Mrs. Wiggins continued, undaunted. "I'll cut back on the sugar and add twelve grams of soy protein and the minimum daily requirement of all the essential vitamins and minerals. Mothers — and kids — will love them."

"That's nice, dear," Mr. Wiggins said sleepily. "I'll take two dozen." The words were barely out of his mouth when he began to snore loudly.

Mrs. Wiggins never did go back to sleep that night. She was far too excited. She was convinced her inner self had spoken to her. She had no idea it was McGrowl who had orchestrated the entire affair.

By the time it was morning, she had already attempted to make Momsicles half a dozen times without success. "Too sweet," she had said, or "Needs more lemon rind," or "Not creamy enough."

In no time at all, Thomas and McGrowl were flying down the stairs, hair combed and paws washed, expecting to find the usual array of breakfast treats waiting to be savored. They discovered, instead, an exhausted Mrs. Wiggins lying fast asleep at the kitchen table. Mr. Wiggins was upstairs getting dressed. Roger was already at his early morning basketball warm-up.

At McGrowl's telepathic urging, Thomas quietly took out one of the cookbooks and opened it to just the right page. McGrowl instructed the boy to circle the most important part of the recipe, the part that Mrs. Wiggins had failed to notice. The part that ensured a long-lasting, perfectly frozen Momsicle every time. And then Thomas and McGrowl hurried off to school.

When she woke up several minutes later and found the cookbook opened to just the right recipe, Mrs. Wiggins was so groggy she assumed it was she who had come upon the missing instructions. She quickly followed them, creating, at last, the prototype for the perfect Momsicle.

When Mr. Wiggins entered the room, she had just completed her daunting task. Her usually spotless kitchen looked like a war zone. Mixing bowls, measuring spoons, and eggbeaters were everywhere. Spilled Jell-O was caked around the edges of the counter, and the floor was a sticky mess.

Before Mr. Wiggins could say a word, Mrs. Wiggins quickly handed him one of the frozen treats. He took a bite. Then another. The grin on his face was worth a thousand compliments. He immediately agreed that the idea for Momsicles was a sound one. "And a delicious one, too," he added.

Mr. Wiggins generously suggested that his advertising agency handle the publicity and marketing. He even proposed that Mrs. Wiggins herself pose as the satisfied Mom on the package. "We'll call you Mrs. Momsicle. You'll be famous. You could have your own syndicated talk show, maybe even open a restaurant." His eyes sparkled as he sipped his coffee. "Maybe a chain of restaurants."

"You'd better get to work, honey," Mrs. Wiggins exclaimed, looking at her watch. "You're fifteen minutes late already! We're not a multinational corporation yet, you know," she joked.

Mr. Wiggins gave her a big kiss, threw on his overcoat, and raced out the door. Mrs. Wiggins sat at the table and contemplated her rosy future.

CHAPTER NINE
Watch Out for Curves

Thomas sat in second period English class, trying to get Violet's attention. She was sitting next to Binky. The two of them were busily passing notes back and forth. Miss Thompson looked as if she were about to explode.

"Psst, psst," Thomas whispered, trying to warn his friend. It was too late. Miss Thompson had shut her book and was already out of her seat and halfway to Violet's desk. Miss Thompson only got out of her seat when she was really mad.

"Miss Schnayerson, would you please describe the relationship between Huckleberry Finn and Becky Thatcher?" the teacher asked, peering down ominously at Violet.

"Umm," Violet began, stalling for time, "the relationship between Huckleberry Finn and Becky Thatcher?"

"That is correct," Miss Thompson replied stonily.

Violet was supposed to have read the first two chapters of *Tom Sawyer* last night but had been too busy trying on clothes with Binky to even open the book. "I'll be honest with you, Miss Thompson."

"I think that would be a really good idea," said Miss Thompson.

"I have absolutely no idea because I haven't started reading the book yet, but I will tonight," Violet said. "I promise."

Miss Thompson returned to her desk, shaking her head. "I don't know what's gotten into you, Violet Schnayerson, but I hope that whatever it is gets out of you quickly," she said as she sat down and opened her book again.

Thomas knew exactly what had gotten into Violet. She was suffering from Binky-itis. A condition that seemed to be affecting much of the middle school, and even some of the ninth-graders. After class, Thomas cornered Violet in the hallway.

"Miss Thompson was really upset, Violet," he began. "Up until this week, you were one of her favorite students. I'm worried about you. I mean, Binky's really nice, but . . ."

"Everything's fine, Thomas," Violet interrupted. "I don't know what you're talking about." And then she hurried off to join Binky in the library. Violet was so late for math class that afternoon that Mr. Denby gave her a demerit. Even Sally Beeman, the gym teacher, commented on Violet's uncharacteristically sluggish performance on the balance beam, hitherto one of Violet's favorite pieces of equipment.

At recess, Thomas asked Violet if she wanted to look for clues after school with him and McGrowl. "I promised to help Binky and her dad at the Center this afternoon," Violet replied. "I'm sorry. I hope you're not upset." And she really did seem sorry. Just not sorry enough to change her plans.

Thomas wanted to say, "I thought we were friends." Instead, he swallowed his pride and said, "Go. Have fun. Don't worry about Mc-Growl. He'll be fine."

As soon as school was over, Thomas and McGrowl started on their quest. "Sometimes if the trail grows cold, it helps to revisit a crime scene," Thomas told McGrowl as they made their way back to the street near Violet's house where they had discovered the handkerchief in the first place. "I read that in a Hardy Boys mystery once."

McGrowl didn't particularly enjoy the Hardy Boys series. Although he certainly admired many of Franklin Hardy's sleuthing techniques, there weren't half enough dogs in the books for his taste.

Slowly and carefully, McGrowl sniffed the area where they had first come upon the handkerchief, while Thomas searched in every nook and cranny he could find — under bushes, behind trees, inside mailboxes. He even looked under Mr. Spalding's crumbling porch, until the old man himself wobbled out and shook his cane at him, yelling, "Don't go poking around my house, you whippersnapper."

"Sorry, Mr. Spalding," Thomas said politely, scrambling quickly away. And then he noticed a note pinned to a nearby tree. "Uh-oh," Thomas said as he and McGrowl rushed over to it. It was addressed to "The nearsighted Thomas S. Wiggins and his companions." Thomas immediately opened it and began to read.

here's a clue from us to you,
Since clearly you don't know what to do.
We're back, as you have correctly surmised,
Only totally, cleverly, well disguised.
We're under your noses as usual, friend,
don't follow our hair dye, that's a dead end.
Try looking instead where you least expect.
Watch out for a clue that commands respect.
if you're lucky you'll be on our trail very quickly.

if not, your dog will become very sickly.

Yours in crime,

the enemy.

Thomas didn't know what to make of the note, but one thing was certain: Thomas and McGrowl were being closely watched. Smudge and Bunting were practically daring them to find them. And the evil duo was clearly close at hand. Thomas and McGrowl decided to return immediately to the safety of their home, where they could study the note more closely.

"Who are the suspects?" Thomas asked McGrowl after they had ensconced themselves in their room.

McGrowl thought for a moment, scratched his ear with his rear paw, and sent Thomas a telepathic message. *Let's make a list,* he began. Thomas took out a pencil and a pad of paper and started writing down everyone Mc-Growl suggested.

The suspects came in pairs, as McGrowl and Thomas knew Smudge and Bunting never traveled alone. McGrowl quickly began beaming Thomas his telepathic list: *Miss Thompson and Principal Grundy. Mr. Fletch and Miss Rabkin. Mr. Spalding and Miss Beeman.* Each pair of suspects had one thing in common: They all commanded the respect mentioned in the evil duo's poem.

"What about Traci Mueller?" Thomas suggested, thinking of Esther Mueller's eccentric mother. McGrowl nodded his approval, and added that Smudge may have been masquerading as Winston Mueller, Esther's father.

"But Mr. Mueller's so nice," Thomas protested. "He does charity work in his spare time. And he's a class father."

McGrowl replied with characteristic logic

and intelligence: *Everyone's a suspect until they're not.* It made perfect sense. With two villains talented enough to disguise themselves as lampposts if they wanted, *everyone* had to be considered.

"Good thinking," Thomas said, giving McGrowl an approving pat on the head. They continued with their list, but when McGrowl got to Hiram Biddle, Thomas balked once more.

"He can't be a suspect," Thomas protested. "Who's his other half? Not Binky — she's my age! Bunting's too old to pretend to be a girl."

McGrowl nodded in agreement. *You've got me there,* the dog thought.

They decided that they would watch each of the suspects especially closely, although, as McGrowl reminded Thomas, *Just because someone isn't on the list doesn't mean they're* not *a suspect.*

Soon it was time for dinner. Mrs. Wiggins

paused briefly in her Momsicle work to defrost a delicious string bean and potato chip casserole in the microwave, and then she went right back into the kitchen. She and Mr. Wiggins had to deliver ten dozen boxes of Momsicles to local stores by nine o'clock tomorrow morning.

While brushing his teeth and washing his face, Thomas could hear the clanging of pots and dishes in the kitchen as his mother prepared yet another batch. Mr. Wiggins stayed right by her side the whole time, providing moral support and encouragement and washing more dishes whenever the need arose.

"Aren't you kids asleep yet?" Mrs. Wiggins asked when she finally came upstairs and poked her head in the door. Roger was already snoring heavily. Thomas whispered a quiet uh-uh. McGrowl returned to the bed from his vigil at the window.

"Good night, sleep tight, don't let the bedbugs bite," Mrs. Wiggins said. She was out the door again before Thomas stopped her with a quiet, "You forgot."

"I did?" she asked. And then she noticed the hurt look in Thomas's eyes and remembered immediately. "Of course I did. I'm sorry, honey," Mrs. Wiggins replied. She walked back in, kissed Thomas gently on the forehead, and gave McGrowl a soft pat on the head. It was their nightly tradition. "I don't know what's come over me."

"I do," Thomas said. "You're a working mother now. It's okay. Stuart Seltzer's mother is a systems analyst and Sophie Morris's mother is a psychologist. I understand."

But Mrs. Wiggins could tell from the tone of Thomas's voice that he didn't really. "Honey, don't worry," she said comfortingly. "No matter what, I'll always be your mom."

"Can I ask you something?" Thomas whispered.

"Shoot," Mrs. Wiggins said as she sat down on the edge of the bed.

"If you get to be really successful, are you still going to make us dinner?" Thomas asked. "And tuck us in every night?"

"Of course," Mrs. Wiggins replied. She couldn't help but smile.

"And will you still be home every day when I get back from school?" Thomas wondered, a squiggly furrow cutting a worried path across his forehead.

"Absolutely," Mrs. Wiggins said firmly.

"I was sort of hoping you would say that," Thomas said, clearly relieved. "So everything is going to stay *exactly* the same. That's what you're saying. Right?"

McGrowl listened intently to the conversation. He was, after all, nearly six. He wasn't a puppy anymore. Maybe one day he would have a little furry golden-haired offspring of his own to talk to and explain things to. Any pointers he could pick up along the way from Mrs. Wiggins would be greatly appreciated. His large, floppy ears perked up, and he listened carefully to what Thomas's mother was about to say.

"Honey, I would be lying if I said that *nothing* was going to be different. I'll be busier, and we'll all have to work a little harder. From time to time I may even have to do a little traveling. It won't always be easy. But I can tell you this much: Being your mother will always be the most important job in the world to me." Thomas looked up at her with his big brown eyes. "I love you, sweetie," she said as she leaned over and gave him a big hug.

"Thanks, Mom. Same here," Thomas said, returning the hug with all his might. McGrowl looked up at Mrs. Wiggins approvingly. He couldn't have handled the situation better himself.

CHAPTER TEN
Hair Today, Gone Tomorrow

The rest of the week went by quickly. Mrs. Wiggins's Momsicles were an enormous hit. All hundred and twenty boxes practically flew off the shelves on the very first day. Everyone in Cedar Springs had started referring to Mrs. Wiggins as Mrs. Momsicle. The local paper, *Cedar Things,* was preparing a special piece on what they called the "Momsicle Phenomsicle" for the weekend edition.

Violet and Binky remained stuck to each

other like glue. They had even started to dress alike. Violet hardly saw Thomas, except in class. But they didn't speak.

By the end of the week, Salamander fever had reached an hysterical pitch. Banners and pennants were everywhere.

Meanwhile, Thomas and McGrowl continued to search in vain for the evil duo. McGrowl's nose was sore from sniffing, and Thomas's feet were tired from walking all over town. And still no more clues.

Thomas wasn't the least bit surprised when Violet broke her standing Friday afternoon study date with him on account of her "hair date" with Binky. He would have been more surprised if she *hadn't*. "Hair *is* important," Thomas reasoned as they stood outside their lockers on Friday afternoon.

"You're so understanding, Thomas," Violet said.

"Thanks," Thomas replied patiently. In truth, he was actually extremely A, fed up; B, fed up; and C, FED UP.

Thomas and McGrowl spent the rest of Friday afternoon carefully monitoring Mabel Rabkin's activities. After narrowing down the list, she remained the prime Bunting suspect. Miss Rabkin had left school right after the pep rally. As they followed her out the door and down the street, the elderly woman looked nervously about as if she were being followed, which, of course, she was.

She ducked quickly into an alley behind the school, arousing further suspicion. It took McGrowl's super sense of smell to finally locate the woman again, and when they did she nearly eluded them by slipping into a small Hungarian bakery on the far side of town.

What's she doing in there? Thomas wondered.

I don't know, but we're gonna find out, was

McGrowl's speedy reply. In a few minutes, Miss Rabkin emerged with a large bundle and hurried right back to school. Thomas and Mc-Growl followed close behind.

An hour later, when they saw her present the salamander-shaped cake to Coach Trunzo on behalf of the entire faculty at the weekly Friday afternoon staff gathering, Thomas and McGrowl decided it was time to focus their attention in another direction.

While Thomas and McGrowl trailed potential suspects, Violet spent the afternoon with her newfound soul mate. After school, they raided the refrigerator and ate the leftover pizza from Tuesday's study date. Then she and Binky tried on all the clothes in Violet's closet before disappearing into the bathroom, where they proceeded to wash, dry, and style their respective hair.

"Remember, blow-drying can leave a lot of split ends if you're not really careful," Binky warned. She was instructing Violet in some of the finer points of grooming. As she stared at herself in the bathroom mirror, Violet wasn't sure how she felt about her elaborate new hairdo and crimson lipstick. She did, however, enjoy being fussed over by the most popular girl in school.

"I think once you establish a look for yourself, it's really important to stick with it," Binky said as she unrolled the chignon from Violet's notoriously uncooperative hair. "I just don't think this is the way we're going to go," Binky joked as she reached for some more of what she described enthusiastically as "product."

"To tell you the truth, I've never really thought about my hair very much," Violet confided.

"You've got to," Binky insisted as she sprayed even more mousse onto Violet's already saturated curls and began to brush them energetically. "If you don't, who else will?"

"I never really looked at it that way," Violet replied.

"What's the first thing you notice about a person?" Binky asked suddenly.

"Their sense of humor?" Violet asked hopefully.

"Wrong," Binky replied tersely.

Violet took another stab. "The expression on their face?"

"Wrong again. It's their hair. I read a survey in *Teen People.* It says hair is the first thing people notice about a person. Even more than jewelry or body type or anything. Think about it."

Violet *was* thinking about it. She was also beginning to think that the way people looked seemed to be the only thing Binky was interested in. She didn't enjoy talking about anything else. She didn't want to play Monopoly or Clue or Chinese checkers. Binky wasn't even particularly interested in working on next week's assignment on earthworms, which Violet had been looking forward to with great excitement for the entire month.

By six o'clock, Violet had had her hair pulled and pushed and reorganized into so many different shapes she thought it would fall out. She already had a splitting headache, and the two girls hadn't even begun the arduous process of styling Binky's long, braided tresses. Violet hated to admit it, but having the most popular girl in school come to your house for a "hair date" wasn't turning out to be all that it was cracked up to be. She was beginning to feel foolish at how much attention she had paid to Binky all week and how little she had paid to Thomas.

Meanwhile, Alicia was in her room, preparing for Miss Pooch's weekend trip to the Biddles' by packing the bullwawa's favorite blanket and pillow. While everyone was away at the basketball game, Miss Pooch and the rest of the dogs in her class would be reuniting for their refresher weekend package, complete with aromatherapy massage and low-fat, high-fiber spa meals.

Over at the Wigginses', Thomas and Mc-Growl were in the kitchen, poring over the evildoers' poem, hoping for a break in the case. Roger was running around the house in a high state of what Mrs. Wiggins referred to as "basketball-induced insanity." He was frantically searching for his lucky socks. All of Roger's basketball "mojo," as he referred to it, resided in these precious white-and-green-striped knee-high poly-and-cotton socks.

One thing is certain, Thomas thought as his brother tore past him, *Lenny Winkleman didn't take them.*

"Honey, I think your chances of finding

them in the refrigerator are minimal," Mrs. Wiggins said as Roger rummaged through every nook and cranny in the kitchen. He absolutely had to find those socks or the Stevenson Salamanders were doomed to failure.

Thomas decided to take a break from his detective work and went into the den to phone Violet. He and his best friend hadn't said three sentences to each other since Monday, the beginning of what Thomas now referred to as LWV, or Life Without Violet. He was absolutely determined not to let her know how much he missed her. When Violet picked up the receiver, Thomas took a deep breath.

"Oh, hi," Thomas said as though he were surprised Violet had picked up her own phone. "It's you."

"What's up?" Violet asked casually, careful not to let Thomas know how happy she was to hear from him.

"Well, I wanted to ask you this, um, emergency science question, um, and then I've gotta go." It was a poor excuse but the best one Thomas could think of at the time.

"Me, too," Violet replied. In the background, Binky's powerful hair dryer was roaring like a motorboat. Binky had brought along not only her own dryer but an entire collection of beauty products, including a curling iron and a professional manicurist's set.

"You have an emergency science question, too?" Thomas asked, surprised.

"No, I mean I have to go. I'm doing all this really cool stuff."

"Yeah, me, too," Thomas lied. "Like what?"

"Oh, you know, like trying on lipstick, painting our nails, blowing our hair dry — stuff like that." Violet did her best to sound happy and excited. In truth, she was neither. Doing nothing with Thomas was somehow a whole lot more entertaining than doing a million things with the hair-obsessed girl who seemed to have permanently installed herself in her bathroom.

"Binky's still here. She is so-o-o funny. We're having an amazing time. What are you doing?"

"I'm, um, writing this paper on, um, the differences between frogs and toads." Thomas realized it probably didn't sound as amazing as whatever Violet and Binky were doing, but it certainly beat telling the truth. Watching his brother look for his missing lucky socks while unsuccessfully attempting to decipher a poem from two evil strangers was not likely to be considered "cool" on anybody's list of things to do on a Friday night.

"Well, I'd better be going," Violet ventured.

This was Thomas's opportunity to say, "Why don't you come over after Binky leaves, and we can play games and do our homework together and make s'mores for dessert. I've really missed you."

But he was still feeling rejected, so all Thomas said was, "That's nice."

And this would have been a perfect chance for *Violet* to jump in with, "I'm really glad you called. Why don't you come over to my house after dinner? I'm so bored I can't take it any longer. Binky is about as much fun as a bag of rocks."

But Violet had made such a fuss about how special the new girl was, she hated to admit she had made a mistake. So *she* just said, "What did you want to ask me?"

And all Thomas could think of to say was the truth, which was, "I forgot." And with that, the two best friends hung up and stared wistfully at their respective telephones.

Thomas heard cheering from the kitchen. Using his X-ray vision and his highly developed sense of smell, McGrowl had finally located Roger's missing socks. They were tucked neatly into the side pouch of his overnight bag. Exactly where Roger had packed them in the first place.

"You kids asleep yet?" Mr. Wiggins asked tentatively, sticking his head in the bedroom door that night after Thomas, McGrowl, and Roger had all gone to bed. It was his turn to tuck in the boys. He looked around carefully to make sure McGrowl was lying motionless at the foot of Thomas's bed before he stepped all the way into the room.

McGrowl wagged his tail gently, making sure to let Mr. Wiggins know he was happy to see him — but not so happy that he might jump up on him or do something else that would frighten the man.

"Good evening, boys," Mr. Wiggins started. He frequently began his good-night talks as if they were important radio broadcasts. "Your mother thought it would be a good idea if we had a little chat." Roger didn't say a word, so Thomas volunteered a pleasant "Okay, Dad," which was all the encouragement Mr. Wiggins needed to continue.

"Thomas, I know Roger has been getting a lot of attention lately because of the big game. We want to make sure you're not feeling left out," Mr. Wiggins said, patting Thomas's shoulder sympathetically.

"Not at all, Dad," Thomas replied. He was happy *not* to be the focus of everyone's hopes and expectations. He could see what a hard time his brother was having handling all the pressure.

"And, Roger," Mr. Wiggins said, "we want you to know that no matter how the game turns out, we couldn't be prouder of you."

After a long pause, Roger turned over in his bed and began to speak. "Dad, if we don't win tomorrow, I don't know what I'm going to do."

Mr. Wiggins took a deep breath and looked Roger squarely in the eye. "Son, you haven't missed one practice session for the last four years. You excel at something you love to do. As far as I can see, you've already won. Don't let one little championship make you forget that. It's just a game. It's meant to be enjoyed."

And then Mr. Wiggins slowly reached over and patted McGrowl on the head. The dog remained as still as a statue. He tried not to breathe. He knew what an important moment this was for Mr. Wiggins. Then Mr. Wiggins stood back up and addressed Roger softly.

"We're all afraid of something. But that doesn't mean we have to let it get the best of us." And then he quickly left the room. He didn't want Roger to see his hands shaking. But Roger had already noticed, and he was glad he had. If his father could pet a dog, then

Roger could survive tomorrow's game. Roger felt as if an enormous weight had just been lifted from his shoulders.

"'Night, Thomas," he said, and then calmly turned on his side and went to sleep.

"'Night, Roger," Thomas replied. And then he reached over to give McGrowl a good-night hug. McGrowl snuggled his big furry golden head deep into his favorite spot in the crook of Thomas's arm.

In another minute, all three of the room's exhausted occupants were snoring gently and dreaming happily about the big game, and best friends, and bullwawas.

CHAPTER ELEVEN
On the Road Again

"Gatorade?" Mr. Wiggins asked.

"Check," Roger replied.

"Talcum powder, sneakers, extra laces, Handi-wipes?" Mr. Wiggins continued.

"Check, check, check, and check," Roger answered.

Content that Roger had, indeed, remembered to pack everything he needed for the big game, Mr. Wiggins pulled the car out of the driveway and started humming the school pep song, "Stevenson, We Love You." Soon

Roger, Thomas, and even Mrs. Wiggins had joined in the chorus and were singing happily away. Even McGrowl took part in the merriment by barking at appropriate intervals.

The motel where they were staying didn't allow dogs. At Mrs. Schnayerson's suggestion, McGrowl would be spending a special "spa" weekend at the Biddles'. It had actually been Binky's idea. She had generously volunteered to look after McGrowl while the Wigginses were away.

Mr. Wiggins would stop at the Biddles' to drop off the excited golden retriever, before picking up Lane Castleman, Stevenson's prized center, and embarking on the ninety-minute trip to Elwood.

McGrowl was looking forward to squeezing in a little quality time with Miss Pooch somewhere in between her obedience classes and his massages. McGrowl's specially designed weekend boarding package included several luxurious spa treatments as well as what Binky had rapturously described as "five-star dining for the four-footed diner."

After the Wigginses stopped at the Biddles' — and Thomas bid McGrowl a hearty farewell — they drove on to Lane's house. Lane came bounding out the doorway, and hopped eagerly into the station wagon. Lane's parents were away on a business trip, so he was grateful for the ride to the game.

Lane and his family had recently moved to Cedar Springs from Rapid City. Lane was one of the most popular boys in twelfth grade. As if being a tall, good-looking star athlete weren't enough, he constantly surprised everyone with his modesty and his wacky sense of humor.

As the group of merry travelers sped eastward along Route 66 toward Elwood, they began to sing camp songs. They started with the signature tune of Mr. Wiggins's beloved Camp Horseshoe. "Hail to the forest, hail to the streams, hail, hail, Camp Horseshoe, camp of my dreams."

They sang a rousing rendition of "I've Been Working on the Railroad," several choruses of "I've Got Sixpence," and one of Mrs. Wiggins's personal favorites, "My Name Is Yon Yonson, I Come from Wisconsin, I Work in the Lumber Mills There."

Thomas looked out the window as he sang and thought about Violet. He wondered whether she was on her way to the game as well. He thought about Roger and hoped he would do well in the game.

But most of all, he thought about McGrowl. This would be the first time the dog had ever been away from the Wigginses since he had come to live with them. Thomas hoped his dog wouldn't be lonely.

And then Lane Castleman broke into a loud

chorus of "Hats Off to Thee, O Cranston," interrupting Thomas's reverie.

"What's that?" Thomas wondered aloud.

"My old school song," Lane replied.

"Aren't you from Rapid City?" Thomas asked.

"Sure," Lane said, and continued singing.

"Somebody in my grade comes from there. Binky Biddle. Ever hear of her?" Thomas wondered.

Lane thought for a moment, then shook his head. "Don't think so."

"She went to Jefferson Memorial," Thomas added.

"Jefferson Memorial? Cranston is the only school in town. I never even heard of Jefferson Memorial," Lane said with absolute conviction.

"That's funny," Thomas said. It *was* funny. He distinctly remembered that Binky said she came from Rapid City and attended Jefferson Memorial. She had called it "Jeff." He was absolutely certain.

"I'll show you our yearbook sometime," Lane said proudly. "It's called the *Cranium.* It's really neat. It looks like a big skull." And then he resumed singing his school song, "We're never avaricious, our mealtimes are nutritious, we always wash our dishes."

I'm sure there's a perfectly logical explanation for this, Thomas thought as he looked out the window and watched the cars whizzing by.

The Wigginses' car arrived at last at Elwood High. Thomas dashed out and ran across the parking lot and into the gymnasium to look for Violet. "Never realized Thomas cared so much about basketball," Mr. Wiggins said as he and Mrs. Wiggins dropped off Roger and Lane at the players' entrance.

While Mr. and Mrs. Wiggins took their seats,

Thomas spotted Violet, who had just arrived and was eagerly looking for him. "Where's Binky?" Thomas asked, as he elbowed his was over to her.

"She's helping her dad," Violet replied. "And to tell you the truth, it's okay with me."

That and the look of happiness Violet had given him when she first saw him filled Thomas with relief. Violet was clearly no longer under the spell of Binky Biddle. "I'm glad," Thomas replied. "There's something strange about that girl."

"Tell me about it," Violet agreed, remembering the endless hours of hairstyling. Suddenly, a voice blared over the loudspeaker.

"Take your seats, please, the game is about to begin." A roar went up from the excited crowd as it began to push its way farther into the gymnasium. Thomas and Violet were carried helplessly along in the crush. A little first-grader spilled his soda all over Violet, and the syrupy mess formed a long horizontal stain across the front of her new overalls.

"Sorry, ma'am," the boy said earnestly to Violet. She couldn't help but smile as she pulled a handkerchief out of her pocket and quickly started dabbing at the stain.

"What's that?" Thomas asked, panic rising in his voice.

"Just a handkerchief. What's the big deal?" Violet said, rubbing the cola stain with all her might.

"Where'd you get it?" Thomas asked, unable to take his eyes off the beige square. The crowd was so raucous he practically had to yell to be heard.

"It's Binky's. She left it at my house yesterday," Violet replied. "Is something wrong?"

Thomas took the dripping linen square from Violet and examined it closely. It looked exactly like the handkerchief Thomas and McGrowl had discovered on the lawn near

Violet's house. Except, on this handkerchief, someone had gone to considerable trouble to remove the incriminating initials.

"There sure is!" he shouted hoarsely. "Look at that."

He showed Violet where the initials *GB* had been neatly removed from the lower right-hand corner. The remaining imprint of the letters clearly revealed to whom the handkerchief belonged.

In a most amazing transformation, Gretchen Bunting had ingeniously disguised herself as none other than Binky Biddle. The long braid, the rosy cheeks, even the girlish obsession with hair and clothing, were all a part of the miraculous deception. She had probably never even been to Rapid City, so she had invented "Jeff."

Binky Biddle simply didn't exist. She was a creation of Gretchen Bunting's demented imagination. And it was likely that Hiram Biddle was another one of Smudge's brilliant impersonations.

"Oh, no!" Violet gasped.

"Oh, yes!" Thomas exclaimed just as the referee blew his whistle and hurled the opening ball into the air. Lane Castleman and Phil Muncie leaped into the air to retrieve it as the crowd began to chant, "Go, go, go!"

Thomas sent McGrowl an urgent telepathic message: *Get out of there. Now. You are in terrible danger.* There was no response. Thomas tried again. Still no response. By now, Violet and Thomas had arrived at the Salamander bleachers and taken their seats.

"McGrowl's in trouble. We've gotta get back," Thomas whispered frantically into Violet's ear. But it was clear that until the game was over, there was absolutely no way of returning to Cedar Springs.

CHAPTER
TWELVE
Spellbound

McGrowl never received Thomas's telepathic warning. Smudge had lined the walls
of the entire Biddle Center with a thin coating
of lead, effectively blocking the boy's signals.

Spa services were in the basement. Binky
led the way. McGrowl happily followed her
down the stairs and into the well-lighted,
cheerful room. The walls were painted a soothing green, and gentle music was piped in
through wall-mounted speakers. The comforting aroma of dried herbs and vanilla bean
hung in the air, creating an aura of well-being

and relaxation. McGrowl decided he was going to have a wonderful time.

He immediately spotted Miss Pooch and the rest of her classmates, locked up securely in a series of cages lined up against the wall.

How quiet and well behaved they all seem, McGrowl thought. The music and the odors did seem to be doing their job. Rumpy, Fluffy, and Franklin all sat at relaxed attention. Even Willie was resting peacefully with his head in his bowl. Miss Pooch gazed contentedly out at McGrowl, not even bothering to hurl herself against the bars of her cage. She didn't appear to recognize him.

That's strange, McGrowl thought. He was unaware of the fact that every one of the dogs had been successfully hypnotized by Hiram Biddle, who was none other than Milton Smudge. Miss Pooch and the others hadn't learned obedience. They were all in a trance.

Just then, Bunting-as-Binky came over,

carrying a dish of steak, medium well, smothered in onions, with mashed potatoes on the side. She placed the dish in front of the dog. McGrowl wagged his tail happily as he tore into the meal. He had no idea that spa cuisine could be so delicious. He was so excited he failed to notice that his food had been laced with an odorless, flavorless muscle relaxant.

Smudge wasn't taking any chances. He had added a special treat to McGrowl's food to make him an easier candidate for hypnosis. Smudge would wait until the drug took effect and then put the dog into a nice, deep, long-lasting trance. McGrowl wouldn't even know what was happening to him.

In each of his previous efforts to capture McGrowl, Smudge had resorted to the use of electromagnets. Although only electromagnets were capable of zapping McGrowl's powers, something always went wrong with the cumbersome devices. The time had come for a new approach.

When Smudge had come across the ad for the six-week home study course entitled Advanced Hypnosis for Fun and Profit, he'd signed up immediately. He'd been an excellent student, focusing his energies on the hypnosis of animals. He soon realized how well he could use his newly acquired skills in his plan to capture McGrowl.

He had promptly moved into Thomas's neighborhood and set up shop as Hiram Biddle. As a dog trainer, Smudge knew he could practice his hypnosis skills daily, honing them until the moment he would face off against McGrowl. And, in disguising himself as Biddle, Smudge knew he would win the trust and respect of every dog owner in town. Hiram Biddle was the unique creation of Smudge's twisted imagination — an irresistible combination of Captain Kangaroo and Mister Rogers. No wonder the children loved him.

Gretchen Bunting had posed as his popular daughter in her most elaborate and challenging impersonation to date. As Binky Biddle, Bunting had infiltrated Thomas and Violet's world without arousing the slightest suspicion. Bunting had total access to all sorts of McGrowl information. She knew when he was coming and when he was going. Even Smudge had to admit Bunting's creation was a stroke of evil genius.

When Mrs. Wiggins had called Mrs. Schnayerson on Friday to discuss pre-game festivities, she'd happened to mention that the motel in Elwood didn't allow dogs, and McGrowl needed a place to stay. Mrs. Schnayerson had hung up and immediately told Violet who immediately told Binky. Binky looked up casually from her makeup mirror and innocently suggested McGrowl spend the night at the Biddle Center for a complimentary "get acquainted" visit.

"He'll love it," Binky enthused. " I'll get my dad to throw in a couple of free massages, and our delicious spa meal package." Mrs. Schnayerson was so excited she called Mrs. Wiggins right back and told her about Binky's generous offer. Bunting was so excited she nearly threw her wig in the air and revealed her true identity. Neither Thomas nor Violet suspected a thing. Thomas led his beloved friend into the fiendish trap without a moment's hesitation.

Binky Biddle had been a difficult disguise to maintain. The elaborate hair and makeup took Bunting several hours to apply. Squeezing her enormous size eleven feet into Binky's delicate size seven Pumas hurt so much it brought tears to her eyes, but it had been worth every painful moment. Worldwide domination was so close, Smudge and Bunting could practically taste it.

*   *   *

Halftime was about to begin. Roger had scored fifteen points so far and made only one foul. Stevenson was leading Hoover High thirty to twenty-two.

Thomas and Violet watched in a daze. They kept looking at their watches. Fortunately, Mr. and Mrs. Wiggins were so wrapped up in the game they hadn't noticed that the two friends had remained as quiet as mice during the entire first half.

An excited hush fell over the crowd and the lights dimmed, plunging the gymnasium into total darkness.

"How much longer?" Violet asked Thomas.

"Too long," said Thomas. He couldn't imagine why McGrowl hadn't returned any of his telepathic messages. He was so worried, he didn't know what to do.

Suddenly, the lights came up again and the

crowd let out a cheer as fifteen Salaman-drettes, Stevenson High's cheerleading squad, filed onto the court. Alicia Schnayerson was captain and drilled her girls as if they were try-ing for an Olympic gold medal. They took to the court in salamander formation, in their gold lamé uniforms and green lizard hoods.

"They're green, they're cute, they love to jump and shoot! Hippos, watch out! They're gonna kick your snout! Goooooo SALAMAN-DERS!" The Salamandrettes threw one another into the air with a series of somer-saults and cartwheels, landing in a pyramid. Alicia balanced at the very pinnacle, scream-ing and cheering at the top of her lungs.

"Isn't there anybody back home we could call? Maybe someone could go to the Biddles' and check on McGrowl?" Thomas asked.

"Everybody's here," Violet replied sadly.

Art Morris tapped Thomas and Violet on the

shoulders and asked them to be quiet. "There's a show going on here, you know," he pointed out indignantly.

The band joined the cheerleaders out on the floor. The crowd rose from the bleachers — all except Thomas and Violet — and joined in a deafening chorus of "O Stevenson, O Stevenson, We Love Your Hallowed Halls." By the end of the song, several audience members were overcome with emotion and had to be helped out of the stands and re- moved to the first aid area.

At last, the band played its final notes and walked off the court, followed by the Sala- mandrettes, skipping and leaping in a flurry of pom-poms. The overwrought fans sat back down as the players came back out onto the court. The whistle tweeted shrilly, and the game resumed.

* * *

IT'S A DOG-EAT-DOG WORLD

Smudge sat right down on the floor next to McGrowl and began to speak. *How friendly,* McGrowl thought sleepily as he listened to Smudge's calming tone.

"Look into my eyes. Your lids are growing heavier and heavier. . . ." As he spoke he dangled a silver coin at the end of a long chain right in front of McGrowl's eyes. The dog stared as the shiny object swung like a pendulum, back and forth. McGrowl was feeling so relaxed he could barely stand up. The combination of the drug and Smudge's soothing voice was working beautifully. Back and forth, back and forth.

It didn't even occur to McGrowl that he might be in danger. He assumed that Mr. Biddle was merely preparing him for some more wonderful spa services.

"You are in my power," Smudge droned. "Your limbs are growing weaker and weaker."

At last, Smudge instructed the dog to lie down and go to sleep, and McGrowl did exactly that.

"When you awaken," Smudge continued, "you will do as I command. Do you understand? Bark once for yes and twice for no."

McGrowl barked a groggy yes. Smudge drank in the moment for several long, delicious seconds. Then he spoke in a quiet voice that trembled with emotion, "The dog is in my power. The world is mine." Since the moment the dog had entered his life, he had dreamed of this day. It was almost more than he could bear. The evil man would have shed tears of joy had he known how to cry.

"Don't you mean *ours*? As in, 'The world is *ours*'?" Bunting asked suspiciously from her post by the door.

"Whatever," Smudge begrudgingly conceded. Then he leaped to his feet and ran upstairs to prepare for phase two of his evil plan.

CHAPTER THIRTEEN
Salamanders Rule

The harsh sound of the ref's whistle brought Thomas's and Violet's thoughts back to the game. Thomas looked at the clock. "It's almost over," he whispered to Violet as they returned to their seats.

"Do you think McGrowl's all right?" Violet asked nervously.

After a long pause, Thomas finally responded. "I don't know," he said, shaking his head.

Suddenly, with only seconds remaining on the clock, Lane Castleman stole the ball from

Phil Muncie and dribbled it across the court, passing it back and forth to Roger in a series of dazzling maneuvers. The two players were practically under the basket and Lane was about to make an easy two-pointer, when, suddenly, Daniel Flusser appeared out of nowhere and grabbed the ball from Lane.

Flusser passed to Larry Scissors, who passed back to Muncie, who turned to shoot and ran right into Roger, knocking him to the ground, onto his already weakened ankle. The referees blew their whistles and the coach ran out to see if Roger was okay. Thomas forgot about McGrowl, and worried about his brother.

The referee immediately declared an intentional foul. The crowd cheered ecstatically. As he limped back onto the court, Roger rubbed his ankle and hobbled slowly over to the free throw line. A hush fell over the crowd as Roger prepared to make his first shot.

Roger was exhausted. He was in pain. He

looked around at the crowd nervously. The entire game was riding on his shoulders. If he made both of his shots, his team would win the championship. If he didn't, they would lose. It was as simple as that.

"Don't think about winning or losing," he told himself, trying to recall his father's exact words. Suddenly, he pictured Mr. Wiggins in his room last night. He was leaning over and patting McGrowl.

And then he heard his father saying, "We're all afraid of something, but that doesn't mean we have to let it get the best of us." Roger relaxed immediately. He was in the middle of a basketball court, his favorite place on earth. How could he possibly be nervous? All thoughts of winning or losing went away, and he realized how much he was enjoying himself.

He smiled, winked at the crowd, and without even thinking, made two of the neatest, cleanest free throws anyone could have imagined. *Swoosh, swoosh.* The game was over in an instant.

As the fans cheered and rushed to pick up Roger and carry him on their shoulders, Thomas and Violet stared at the clock. Time was running out. If they didn't get back soon, it might be too late.

"And that's it for the big game, folks," Wally Flamm said, looking into the television camera as the last excited Salamander fan filed out of the gymnasium. "And what a game it was! I'd like to take a moment to remind you that the last quarter of this evening's entertainment was brought to you by the makers of Momsicles, 'a healthy treat you'll love to eat.'"

Mr. and Mrs. Wiggins looked at each other and grinned proudly. Their son was a hero, and Momsicles were selling so well locally that by the end of the month distribution would widen to include most of Northern Indiana, including Bloomington and greater downtown Gary.

The crowd was still screaming and yelling as Thomas and his exhausted family approached their car in the parking lot. Thomas knew that unless he thought fast, they'd head for the motel, and he wouldn't have a chance of rescuing McGrowl.

"Oh my gosh!" Thomas exclaimed. "I think I left all of the lights on in my room."

"Are you sure?" his mother asked anxiously. "Think hard."

Thomas knew he hadn't left a single light burning. But he was desperate. He couldn't stay in Elwood another minute. He had to find out if McGrowl was all right. "I'm absolutely positive," he replied.

Thomas had come up with a perfect excuse. He might as well have told his parents he had left a campfire burning on the living room rug, as to say he had left one light on in his room — let alone the entire lot of them. His father had a phobia about faulty wiring.

"Kids, we're gonna have to go straight home," Mr. Wiggins announced to Roger and Lane as he put on his driving gloves. Suddenly, Violet appeared out of nowhere, and waved an awkward "hello."

"Can Violet drive back with us?" Thomas asked. "Her family's decided to go back to Cedar Springs, too."

"Absolutely," Mr. Wiggins said cheerfully.

"Thanks," Violet said gratefully as she and the rest of the little group piled into the car.

"Roger, honey, I hope you're not too disappointed we can't stay tonight," Mrs. Wiggins said quietly. She knew he had been looking forward to a special night of celebration with his teammates in Elwood.

"Yeah, Rog, I'm really sorry," Thomas added.

But Roger wasn't the least bit upset. He

was still reliving his amazing victory. Mr. Wiggins was secretly relieved to return to the comfort of his own bed. He found the Cozy Cabin Motel neither comfortable nor cozy. And Mrs. Wiggins looked forward to whipping up a few batches of Momsicles before going to sleep.

As they whizzed quickly along the highway, Lane and Roger slept soundly while Mr. and Mrs. Wiggins went over the entire game point by point and Thomas and Violet stared out the window at the night sky, counting the seconds until they got to McGrowl.

CHAPTER FOURTEEN
Help Is on the Way

Miss Pooch shook her scrawny little neck and scratched energetically at her collar with one of her paws. She had just awakened from her hypnotic trance and was surprised to find herself in Smudge's basement. Her eyelids fluttered gently, and, in a moment, she was fully alert. She looked around, confused. *Where am I?* she wondered.

And then it all came back to her. The girl with the long braid and the big man with the doughy hands had put her into a cage. She didn't like them. They were always ordering her around. She thought about how good it would feel to bite them. She remembered how the nasty man had tried to make her go to sleep. She had put up a fight. After a long struggle, she had given in.

But Miss Pooch had a will of iron and was a poor candidate for hypnosis. She had fallen only into the lightest of trances. She immediately caught the scent of McGrowl. Her nose told her that the dog had been in the room, and recently.

The bullwawa barked as loudly as she could, which was very loud, indeed. It was a high-pitched, irritating, trance-shattering kind of bark. It was a bark of warning, and it announced her readiness to tangle with anyone who dared try to stop her.

Smudge and Bunting couldn't hear the bullwawa. They were upstairs, preparing McGrowl for the final phase of their terrible plan.

"Don't jostle him, you'll wake him from his

trance, you fool," Smudge grunted angrily. Bunting was struggling to carry the sleeping McGrowl through the attic, toward a winding stairway that led to the roof.

"Gotta rest. Can't go on," Bunting panted breathlessly. The dog was heavy.

"Careful of the beakers," Smudge replied.

The attic was where Smudge did his "creative" work. Beakers bubbling with foul-looking potions lined the counters along the wall. Electromagnets of all shapes and sizes littered the floor, the shelves, and the tables. A blindingly bright operating lamp shone down from the ceiling.

There was a makeup area, with chairs and mirrors and rows and rows of every kind of disguise imaginable. Putty noses and false chins were lined up on shelves near an assortment of wigs. What looked like a collection of rare moths was actually a variety of tiny eyebrows and mustaches pinned care-fully to a small bulletin board marked FACIAL HAIR. Racks of clothes and hats completed the sinister picture.

Slowly, Bunting dragged her precious cargo up the little stairway to the roof as Smudge taunted her mercilessly. "Faster, slowpoke," he called. "Train leaves in five minutes." Smudge made the sound of a train whistle as he shoved Bunting aside and pushed his way past her, opening the door to the roof.

Right at the highest point of the house, hid-den from view by the eaves, stood Smudge's secret weapon: a small atomic-powered rocket, just big enough for two adults and one golden retriever. Milton Smudge gazed lovingly at his beautiful, gleaming creation.

The rocket was aimed directly at an unnamed destination from which Smudge planned to begin his campaign of global domination.

"Can Thomas come over for hot chocolate?" Violet asked as the Wigginses' car pulled up to the Schnayersons'.

"Forty-five minutes, Thomas," his mother warned. "Not a minute longer."

"Don't worry, son, I'll turn out your lights," Mr. Wiggins called after him. "Thanks, Dad," Thomas called as he ran to the front door. He hoped his father wouldn't be angry when he discovered that all the lights in his room and even the little night-light in the bathroom had been turned off. Violet, whose parents and sister were still on their way back from Elwood, quietly let them in.

As soon as they heard the Wigginses' car pull away, Thomas and Violet came rushing out the front door and started running to the Biddles' as fast as they could.

*　　*　　*

"Oops," Bunting said as she arrived on the roof at last, lost her balance, and tumbled to the ground. She landed with an enormous crash, dropping McGrowl. She rolled to the edge of the roof, barely able to suppress a scream. She clung to the shingles of the roof with her fingertips. "Help me," she moaned weakly.

"What have you done?" Smudge cried. He quickly set about examining McGrowl to see if the dog was still under his spell. He snapped his fingers loudly right under his nose. McGrowl didn't even flinch. "Lucky for you, Bunting," Smudge warned. "That's all I can say."

"Not a 'How are you?'" Bunting hissed in return. "Not a 'Thank you very much for practically killing yourself in the service of evil'?" The woman stuck out her tongue at Smudge.

"You take that back," Smudge roared.

"Will not," Bunting retaliated, taking off her

shoe and throwing it at Smudge. It missed narrowly and rolled off the roof, landing in the front yard with a damp *plop.* Smudge responded by reaching over and grabbing her wig. He pulled it off in one deft motion.

"My hair, my beautiful hair!" she cried. "You know something? You're rotten. To the core. Through and through. In and out. Upstairs and downstairs."

"That's the nicest thing anybody's said to me in weeks," Smudge shot back. And with that the evil duo stopped their bickering, picked up the limp McGrowl, and started strapping him into the rocket.

Miss Pooch continued barking until her four sleepy companions had been awakened from their slumber and joined in the barking as well. Then she started hurling her body against the bars of her cage. She would find McGrowl if it was the last thing she did.

IT'S A DOG-EAT-DOG WORLD

Smudge and Bunting weren't fools. They had outfitted their obedience school and spa with the very latest in restraining devices when they first set up shop. But they hadn't counted on the persistence of the feisty little bullwawa.

Miss Pooch hurled and hurled and refused to give up. Soon the other dogs joined in and started hurling themselves against their cages as well. Pretty soon, the long row of interconnected cages started teetering back and forth until one enormous group hurl caused the entire lot to come crashing to the ground, short-circuiting the electronic closing system.

One by one the doors to the cages sprang open, and Miss Pooch trotted out as if nothing had happened. She was followed by a groggy Fluffy, Rumpy, Willie, and Franklin. The dogs shook themselves and rubbed their paws over their sleepy faces until they were thoroughly awake and ready for anything.

Miss Pooch led the search party. Her tiny

legs were a blur as she hurried up the stairs to explore the living room.

By now McGrowl was tightly strapped into the rocket on the roof. Smudge was leaning against the chimney, reading aloud from a checklist of important things to do before taking off. "Engage throttle?"

"Check," Bunting replied as she hovered anxiously over the aircraft, shining her flashlight and clicking her heels efficiently. She enjoyed any form of military activity.

"Restrainer flaps?"

"Check," Bunting answered as she reached into the bowels of the engine and unsnapped the heavy metal bands that held the flaps snugly in place.

"Sandwiches, Ring-Dings, juice boxes, pretzels . . ." Smudge was halfway through the items before he realized that Bunting had run out of paper and had used the checklist to write down her grocery list.

Meanwhile, Miss Pooch was following McGrowl's scent over to the stairs that led to the attic. Her spiky little head bobbed up and down energetically as she explored every inch of the floor.

At first, Rumpy and Fluffy insisted on batting around a jar of liver treats they had found on the coffee table until Miss Pooch rounded them up with a swift growl, punctuated by an emphatic snarl.

Willie and Franklin were more obedient but moved more slowly than the domineering bullwawa would have liked, so she herded the recalcitrant animals by running around them in quick circles and nipping gently at their legs. Soon, all five dogs were moving swiftly and silently up the stairs in relentless pursuit of McGrowl and his captors.

CHAPTER FIFTEEN
Blastoff

Thomas and Violet carefully tiptoed up to the Biddles' house. The door was ajar, and every light in the place had been turned off. Slowly, they entered. An eerie sense of stillness filled Violet with dread. Thomas reached into his pocket and touched his magic rock for good luck. His mother had given it to him, and he never left the house without it. He took out his mini flashlight and shined it around the room.

"There's no one in here," Thomas whispered, his heart sinking.

"Over here," Violet said, spotting the staircase. Together, she and Thomas crept down the creaky stairs to the basement.

"Shhh," Thomas warned.

"I'm scared," Violet confessed.

"Me, too," Thomas replied. A shaft of moonlight shone through a basement window. "McGrowl isn't here," Thomas said, confirming their worst fears.

"Neither is Miss Pooch," Violet whispered in return. "Where do you think they went?"

All of a sudden, the floor creaked, and Thomas motioned for Violet to be quiet. The two children stood still, waiting to see what was going to happen.

"Just the wind," Violet said after a moment.

Then Thomas spotted something on the floor. "Look," Thomas whispered. "There's his collar." Thomas held up the familiar brown leather band. McGrowl's ID tags jangled softly. "They must have taken it off" —

Thomas took a deep breath — "before they took him away." He placed the collar gently in his backpack and started tiptoeing back up the stairs.

"Wait a minute. I think I hear something!" Violet exclaimed. Thomas turned off his flashlight, and they proceeded cautiously up the stairs. Finally, at the top of the steps, right before the entryway to the roof, they came upon Miss Pooch and her four furry companions.

Unfortunately, Rumpy was so excited to see Thomas and Violet that she let loose one of her earsplitting, gut-wrenching welcome barks, and the other dogs joined in.

On the roof, Smudge heard the commotion and frantically jumped into the aircraft, motioning for Bunting to join him. He began to strap himself in.

But then the frantic yapping of five eager dogs filled the night air as Miss Pooch's gang rushed onto the roof, followed by Thomas and Violet. "Charge!" Thomas cried, and the dogs made straight for the rocket.

"There's nothing you can do to stop us, so don't even try," Smudge hissed in a voice so menacing even Miss Pooch stopped in her tracks. The other dogs all turned to Thomas to see what they should do next. Miss Pooch stared numbly at McGrowl. She couldn't bear to see him tied up and defenseless. She began to whine uncontrollably.

"Where are you taking McGrowl?" Thomas asked bravely, eyeing his poor dog strapped helplessly into the rocket.

"That's for me to know and you to find out," Smudge taunted as a whirring sound suddenly started up. Bunting couldn't suppress a gleeful smile. All they had left to do was to start the ignition that would fire up the engines, and Smudge, Bunting, and McGrowl would disappear forever.

"I thought you were my friend," Violet said

to the woman beside Smudge who still looked like Binky.

"*Binky* was your friend," Bunting said as she proceeded to peel off her incredibly life-like mask. "But then, she wasn't real." Violet felt a shudder run through her as Binky started to disappear right before her eyes, revealing Gretchen Bunting in her place.

First, the round rosy cheeks turned gray and hollow, then the upturned nose became a crooked, wide protrusion, and finally, Bunting removed her bright blue contact lenses, and a pair of haunted pale green eyes stared back at Violet.

"This is the real me," she gloated. "Ain't I something?" Bunting grinned a wicked, toothless grin. Evidently, being a force of evil involved poor dental hygiene. At least in Bunting's case.

"I think you forgot something," Thomas ventured, pointing to one of the far eaves of the roof. It was a last-ditch attempt to distract Smudge.

"That is the oldest trick in the book," Smudge smirked as he struggled to pull down a large heat-protective visor over the front of the craft. The whirring sound from the engine was growing in intensity.

"No, really," Violet added. She pointed vigorously, desperately trying to stall Smudge. She was so convincing even Willie and Fluffy looked to see what was going on.

But not Smudge. "I'm not buying," he replied smugly. "But you're still selling."

"You're awful," Thomas snapped.

"If you think I'm bad now, wait until I take over the world," Smudge gloated. "I'll show you awful." Meanwhile, Miss Pooch started creeping silently closer to the rocket.

"You'll never make it off this roof with Mc-Growl," Thomas went on, undeterred.

"Like I don't have the ignition switch in my

hands at this very moment," Smudge growled. He lifted up a small rectangular plastic box and waved it in the air gleefully. In a second, Thomas and Violet realized, there would be nothing anyone could do to stop him.

Suddenly, Miss Pooch started wailing like a banshee and threw herself into the air. She flew directly at Smudge, knocking the device out of his hands. Then she pounded on Mc-Growl's face with her small but muscular fore-arms before tumbling onto the sloping roof.

McGrowl began to stir. Miss Pooch had awakened him. Bunting reached down, grabbed the remote control, and with an au-dible *click,* the ignition was engaged. There was no turning back.

The engines began to scream. Smudge grabbed his trusty coin and started swinging it in front of McGrowl, desperately attempting to put the dog securely back into his trance. "Your eyelids are growing heavy," Smudge muttered.

IT'S A DOG-EAT-DOG WORLD

As Smudge spoke, Violet quickly removed from her small purse the mirror Binky had given her yesterday with the advice, "Never leave the house without a mirror in your pocket and a smile on your face." The mirror, at least, was proving to be a good idea. Violet handed it to Thomas, who immediately got the point and quietly placed himself behind McGrowl. He casually held the mirror up so that it reflected Smudge.

"Look into my eyes," Smudge continued. Without knowing it, he was inadvertently hypnotizing both himself and Bunting. Ever vain, she was foolishly looking into the mirror to straighten her wig, which she had hastily put back on in preparation for her journey. "You are getting sleepier and sleepier," Smudge went on in a slow, heavy voice, putting both himself and Bunting deeper into a trance.

McGrowl did everything he could to stay awake. He counted backward. He recited the

Pledge of Allegiance. He thought about how grateful he was for Thomas, Violet, and the brave Miss Pooch, who was still sitting where she had landed, busily licking the paw she had injured in the fall.

As Smudge and Bunting grew sleepier, Thomas easily grabbed the coin out of Smudge's hands and dangled it right in front of the evil duo's eyes. "When you wake up, you will not remember who you are or where you came from," Thomas intoned, swinging the coin slowly back and forth. And then he added one more crucial command: "You will forget McGrowl ever existed."

Both Smudge and Bunting mumbled a sleepy "Yes, sir" as their eyelids fluttered shut.

McGrowl was fully awake now. He bit through his seat belt in one easy crunch and leaped out of the rocket. The roof started to shake so hard Thomas was afraid the house would fall down. Violet held her ears as a blinding flash filled the air and the rocket rose up violently from the roof and started arcing its way through the night sky, carrying its evil passengers far, far away.

Six excited dogs barked long and loud at the spacecraft as Thomas and Violet exchanged smiles of relief. McGrowl bounded up to receive a huge hug. Thomas looked at his watch.

"Gotta be home in ten minutes, or my goose is seriously cooked," Thomas remarked. Then he picked up a surprisingly docile Miss Pooch and rushed off with Violet to return the other dogs to their proper homes.

CHAPTER SIXTEEN
Happy Ending

Thomas and Violet dropped off Rumpy, Franklin, Willie, and Fluffy with the hurried explanation that the dogs had completed their studies early. The four different owners couldn't have been more proud. Then, Thomas and McGrowl dropped off Violet and Miss Pooch.

"Guess I'll see you tomorrow," Thomas said to Violet.

"Guess so," Violet replied as Thomas turned to leave. "Thomas?" Violet asked. Thomas turned back immediately. "Could you believe it when Binky turned into Bunting right before our eyes?"

"How about when Miss Pooch attacked Smudge and foiled his entire plan?" Thomas replied.

"Amazing," Violet agreed. "Wanna look for earthworms tomorrow?"

"I thought you'd never ask," Thomas said, happily. And then he smiled broadly at Violet, who happened to be smiling broadly right back at him.

I smell cooked goose was the only telepathic message McGrowl had to send. Thomas was off and running.

Once they got home, he and McGrowl got into bed so quickly they were fast asleep before the Wigginses had a chance to ask them a single question.

The next morning, Thomas and McGrowl accompanied the Schnayersons to the vet. Dr. Minderbinder quickly determined that

Miss Pooch's paw was bruised but not broken. (McGrowl had examined her leg the night before and determined the same thing himself.)

As Dr. Minderbinder finished the general examination, he smiled mysteriously at the Schnayersons, Thomas, and McGrowl. "But there is something I'd like to take another look at."

And then, while everyone held their collective breaths, he poked and prodded Miss Pooch before he finally spoke again.

"Let me be the first to congratulate you, Miss Pooch," Dr. Minderbinder said. Miss Pooch cocked her head to one side and listened attentively. "In one month, you are going to be the proud mother of some happy little puppies."

Mr. and Mrs. Schnayerson looked at each other, stunned. What in the world were they going to do with more little Miss Pooches?

"Couldn't you just die!" Alicia exclaimed.

"My sentiments precisely," Mrs. Schnayerson said under her breath. Thomas and Violet exchanged surprised glances as McGrowl padded right over to Miss Pooch and put a protective paw around her shoulders. He beamed with pride.

"Guess we know who the proud father is," Mr. Schnayerson said, pointing at McGrowl.

"Do you have anything to say for yourself, young dog?" Doc Minderbinder joked.

McGrowl barked happily as Thomas, Violet, and the rest of the Schnayersons leaned over and gave the happy parents-to-be enthusiastic hugs and kisses.

"Maybe they'll take after their father," Mr. Schnayerson said hopefully.

"We'll have one month to find out," Thomas said as everyone turned to look at Miss Pooch. She had her leash in her mouth and was wagging her tail. Motherhood certainly seemed to agree with her. She was already behaving better than she had in years.

That night, Mrs. Wiggins crept into their bedroom and said good night to a sleepy Thomas, Roger, and McGrowl. "Good night, kids and dog," Mrs. Wiggins said softly as she left the room. "Sleep well. You've had a busy week."

You have no idea how busy, Thomas thought. McGrowl couldn't have agreed more. Roger had fallen asleep before his mother had even left the room, still exhilarated and exhausted from yesterday's amazing basketball victory.

As Mrs. Wiggins washed her face and brushed her teeth, she couldn't help but think about how wonderful her life was. *I have a loving husband. Two fantastic children. And the best dog in the world. And now I even have a career. What more could I ask for?*

IT'S A DOG-EAT-DOG WORLD

Little did she suspect that Momsicles were about to become the number one health snack in the country. Mr. Wiggins's life was about to change dramatically as well. He was about to get a promotion and take charge of the entire Momsicle account.

In the boys' bedroom, McGrowl rolled over onto his back, waited for Thomas to scratch his stomach, and thought about how excited he was to become a parent. He would name one of the boy puppies Thomas and one of the girl puppies Violet. He would teach them to be good dogs.

Thomas looked up at the stars on his ceiling. Sirius, the dog star, seemed to be twinkling especially brightly. Thomas thought about how happy he was for McGrowl. He thought about how relieved he was to be rid of Smudge and Bunting once and for all. He thought about how much he enjoyed having Violet back as his best friend.

McGROWL

As Thomas fell asleep, the first snowflakes of the year started falling gently. Soon the pond would be frozen and there would be sledding on Dead Man's Hill. And Christmas presents to make. And four little golden bull-wawa puppies to play with. Which happened to be exactly what McGrowl was dreaming about.

Bob Balaban is a respected producer, director, writer, and actor. He produced and costarred in Robert Altman's Oscar®- and Golden Globe–winning film *Gosford Park,* which was named Best British Film of 2001 at the British Academy Awards. He appeared in *Close Encounters of the Third Kind*, *Absence of Malice*, *Deconstructing Harry*, *Waiting for Guffman*, *Ghost World*, *The Mexican*, and *A Mighty Wind*, among many other films, and appeared on *Seinfeld* several times as the head of NBC. Bob produced and directed the feature films *Parents* and *The Last Good Time*, which won best film and best director awards at the Hamptons International Film Festival. Bob lives in New York with his wife, writer Lynn Grossman, and his daughters, Hazel and Mariah. At the moment, he is canine-less, but he is looking forward to a close encounter with his own actual dog, not just one of the literary kind.

Meet BAD DOG

There's only one way for the baddest dog in town to escape Death Row at the City Pound for Unwanted Canines—volunteer to become the very first mutt on Mars.

If Bad Dog can scrape through basic training, he just might be destined for the Red Planet. But a lot can happen between countdown and take-off. So, will Bad Dog be defending Earth from an alien invasion, or will he be rocketing back to Death Row?

In Stores February 2005

BAD DOG and those Crazee Martians!
by Martin Chatterton

BDT